MORE TALES FROM CHARLETON HOUSE

CHARLETON HOUSE MYSTERY SHORTS

KATE P ADAMS

Copyright © Kate P Adams 2025

The right of Kate P Adams to be identified as the author of this work has been asserted by her in accordance with the Copyright, Designs and Patents Act 1988.

All rights reserved. No part of this publication may be reproduced, transmitted, or stored in a retrieval system, in any form or by any means, without permission in writing from the author, nor be otherwise circulated in any form of binding or cover other than that in which it is published and without similar condition being imposed on the subsequent purchaser.

All characters in this publication, other than those clearly in the public domain, are fictitious and any resemblance to real people, alive or dead, is purely coincidental.

Cover design by Dar Albert

ALSO BY KATE P ADAMS

THE CHARLETON HOUSE MYSTERIES

Death by Dark Roast

A Killer Wedding

Sleep Like the Dead

A Deadly Ride

Mulled Wine and Murder

A Tragic Act

A Capital Crime

Tales from Charleton House

Well Dressed to Die

Death on Display

More Tales from Charleton House

THE JOYCE AND GINGER MYSTERIES

Murder En Suite

Murder in the Wings

*To my friends
Jo Hancox and Becki Scott.
You provided a port in the storm, then gave me a key and access to the
chocolate cupboard.*

CONTENTS

An A-maze-ing Christmas	1
Key to a Killer	13
Chapter 1	14
Chapter 2	19
Chapter 3	21
Chapter 4	25
Chapter 5	29
Chapter 6	33
Chapter 7	36
Chapter 8	40
Chapter 9	43
Epilogue	48
The Letter of the Law	51
Dear Monty: A Christmas Letter	68
The Skeletons of Stone Court	73
- Joyce Brocklehurst	74
- The Duchess of Ravensbury	77
- The Duke of Ravensbury	80
- Mark Boxer	83
Dear Monty: An Update	87
A Private Murder	91
Chapter 1	92
Chapter 2	100
Chapter 3	105
Chapter 4	109
Chapter 5	114
Chapter 6	118
Chapter 7	123
Chapter 8	127
Chapter 9	130
Chapter 10	133
The Joyce and Ginger Mysteries	137
Chapter 1	138

Chapter 2	143
Chapter 3	147
Read a free Charleton House Mystery	151
About the Author	153
Acknowledgements	155

AN A-MAZE-ING CHRISTMAS

'I'm sorry I'm late, I came as quick as I wanted to.'

Joyce reached for the paper cup of mulled wine. 'No glassware, Sophie? I'm horrified. I haven't drunk out of a paper cup since… actually, I don't think I've ever drunk out of a paper cup.'

Mark very much doubted that, but allowed Joyce to maintain her delusion of grandeur. The food truck dispensing festive drinks and snacks was an old Citroën van which wouldn't have looked out of place trundling along a French country road, but was now painted a very smart navy blue, the Ravensbury family crest in gold on the side. Chestnuts were roasting, the smoky aroma filling the air. A vast pan of sweet-smelling hot chocolate was being stirred. Decorations of dried orange slices and cinnamon sticks hung along the top of the hatch. Sophie's staff were wrapped up in scarves and hats, but despite the cold, they smiled and laughed with the visitors and occasionally joined in with the carol singers who were performing in the centre of the stables courtyard.

'Have a mince pie and be grateful you don't have to pay.'

Joyce gave the pie a quick sniff, and then took a large bite, her faux upper-class performance vanishing as she chomped on it like a ravenous beast.

'What? Don't either of you look at me like that. I didn't have any dinner,' she mumbled. 'You wouldn't be happy if I fainted part way round and you had to carry me back.'

Mark was tempted to respond with a cutting remark, but he was aware that they were about to wander along a trail with a number of unlit sections and it would be easy enough for Joyce to commit murder and toss his body into the bushes without anyone spotting. He enjoyed his banter with Joyce, but he didn't have a death wish.

The three friends and colleagues had gathered to explore the Charleton House Christmas Light Trail that wound around the gardens of their place of work. The imposing house was a lavish backdrop to the sounds and sights that would lead visitors through a festive extravaganza.

'Come on, troops.' Mark waved his arm in the direction of the gardens. 'Magic awaits, and we only have an hour or so to cover ourselves in the fairy dust of Christmas.'

'I think you covered yourself in a bit too much, Mark Boxer.'

'Now, now, less of the obvious and unimaginative jokes, please. You can do better than that.'

'It wasn't a joke.'

Mark looked at Joyce quizzically until she touched her top lip.

'What? Oh yes.' He laughed. 'I thought I'd throw myself into the evening.'

'Or more accurately, throw yourself face first into a snowdrift,' mused Joyce as she examined the layer of fake snow that Mark had carefully applied along the top of his rather magnificent handlebar moustache.

'Talking of finishing touches, how do you do it? I'd break my neck.' Sophie nodded in the direction of Joyce's feet as she crunched along the path in a pair of stilettos, their shade of fir green matching her cashmere scarf and leather gloves, which were paired with her long, vibrant red coat. Mark had concluded that she looked like a giant poinsettia.

'Years of practice. I could make it across a desert with dignity if the need arose.'

'And stride across the fires of hell, I'm sure,' said Mark, taking a step to the side, well out of Joyce's reach.

'Now, now, children, it's Christmas. Let's be nice or Santa won't bring either of you any gifts.' Sophie wagged her finger at them both playfully.

The mulled wine kept Mark's fingers warm, the steam rising off it still visible in the cold air. He took a deep breath in and closed his eyes, enjoying the rich woody aroma of cinnamon and cloves before promptly knocking into Joyce whose path he'd strayed into.

'Sorry.'

'Are you wandering around with your eyes closed?'

'No, of course not.' He could see Sophie smirking.

Children were bundled up, running back and forth along the paths, covering two or three times the distance their parents would over the course of the evening. Combine Christmas with vast quantities of sugar and the promise of staying up late, and Sophie could be sure that the profits her café staff would take on mulled wine would be up as parents found a way to cope.

Otherworldly shrieks and laughter echoed up ahead. A small boy let out a deep *ho-ho-ho* into a funnel; in response, the lights in a row of trees rippled and skipped from branch to branch, moving in response to his words. Gold and silver blazed amongst the twigs, lighting up their natural structures, the bare branches becoming ghostly silhouettes before being plunged once more into darkness.

Mark eventually took the place of the child and started an oration.

"'Twas the night before Christmas, when all through the house
Not a creature was stirring, not even a mouse…'

A young girl glared up at him, her stern look making it very clear what she thought of his performance. He kept going for a few more lines until she folded her arms and narrowed her eyes. He stepped away.

'Alright, alright, everyone's a critic.'

A meadow of delicate glistening lights surrounded the Great Pond, the fountain pouring forth watery flames of red, yellow, and orange.

'Look!' shouted Mark, waving at Joyce and pointing in the direction of the fountain. 'Your master is calling.'

'Are you quite done? You really have been sent to test me and I'm concerned I might fail this particular test.'

'Well, you better get some practice in, you're going to have to make it through the whole of Christmas Day in my company.'

Sophie came to a sudden stop. 'I'm sorry, did I hear right?'

'I'm as surprised as you are, Sophie dear, but for some unfathomable reason, I said *yes* when Bill invited me to join their family get together. I neglected to consider that it would mean spending a day in the company of his husband too.' She looked over at Mark, who shrugged.

'I will be the jingle in your bells, the bobble on your beanie, the brandy cream on your pudding. In my company, your Christmas turkey will be filled with the giblets of joy.'

She locked eyes with him and in a single steady tone replied, 'This Christmas, you will drive me crackers.'

'Oh, touché,' cried Mark with delight. 'Christmas Day is going to be so much fun.'

Projections of flowers on paths made for lush carpets of garish colours that swirled hypnotically. Enormous Christmas baubles became igloos to explore. A wisteria tunnel was transformed into a glittering passage of lights and the three friends ambled through it, enjoying pieces of stollen that had appeared from Sophie's pocket, scattering snow-like powdered sugar on the ground.

'Tell me,' said Mark, glancing over at Sophie, 'what's your favourite memory of Christmases past?'

'Easy. Christmas stockings. I always used one of my dad's hiking socks. Big, long, rough things. None of this modern fabric, they were the kind of socks you could imagine Edmund Hillary wearing as he made his way up Everest. I'd lay it on the end of the bed, and then try to go to sleep.

'In the morning, before I had even opened my eyes, I could feel the weight of the heavy, lumpy sock on my feet. If I moved a little, I could hear the wrapping paper rustling against the rough fabric. I would sit up in bed and open the gifts. Amongst all the little presents, there was always an apple and a satsuma – which never got eaten, of course – and chocolate coins. I swear chocolate coins on Christmas morning are the best tasting chocolate ever. But it was the feel of the laden sock resting on my feet that I loved the most. I knew Santa had been. Even when I no longer believed in Santa, for that brief moment, I did.'

Mark looped his arm through Sophie's and the three of them finished walking through the sparkling tunnel in silence.

'Your turn,' said Mark to Joyce as they walked past trees hung with hundreds of twinkling snowflakes that twisted and turned in the breeze. 'Tell us about your most outrageous Christmas.'

Joyce took a deep breath and appeared to be about to refuse to answer. But instead, she said, 'The Orient Express: Rome, Venice, Portofino, and then back to Rome for Christmas Day.'

'Ah! La dolce vita!' exclaimed Mark. 'I bet you looked like a classic Hollywood star, with one of those fancy trunks, fur coat, sunglasses.'

'My dear, I put mere actors into the shade. Also, I didn't wear fur. Well, not real, anyway. The collar and cuff were fake mink.'

'That must have set you back a pretty penny,' said Mark, sounding impressed.

'Not a single penny, pretty or otherwise. Thanks to my double-crossing husband.'

'The surgeon?' asked Sophie.

'Yes, the surgeon. After I booted him out, I happened to find one of his credit cards in the bottom of a drawer and I decided to see if it was still working.'

'You just happened to find it, did you?' asked Mark, sounding deeply suspicious. 'Or did it just happen to find its way into your purse as soon as you discovered what he had been up to and you held on to it until the opportunity for a proper splurge and a touch of revenge arose?'

'You are unfairly suspicious, Mark Boxer.' She sounded put out, sniffed, and then added, 'Well, I might have put it in my purse for safekeeping. I wouldn't have wanted it to go missing again. And anyway, he was dreadful with money. I managed that side of things when we were married. It took him six months to realise that he'd funded my little train ride.'

She cackled. 'Of course, there was nothing he could do. I needed the trip to recover from the trauma of his betrayal, and I had one of the best solicitors my husband's money could buy, so he knew it wasn't worth fighting.' There was a look of real glee on Joyce's face. 'It really was a marvellous Christmas.'

The trio kept walking along paths lit with lanterns, past groups of oversized sparkly deer, until they reached a vast keyboard laid out on the grass in front of a splendid view of Charleton House. They watched as a group of children leapt about. As they landed on a key, a note rang out loud and clear and a section of the building lit up. Each key gave a different note and a different colour on a different part of the house.

The friends stood and watched the musical chaos as the children jumped around and laughter filled the air. Once they had exhausted themselves, they ran off in the direction of a rather chilly looking group of adults, and much to the surprise of Sophie and Mark, Joyce made her way to the keyboard and tapped her foot on a key, then another. Charleton House lit up under her seeming magical powers. She gave a spirited jump to a far key, then spun as she made for another. As a simple rendition of *We Wish You a Merry Christmas* played out under Joyce's feet, the house appeared to have a life of its own, joining in with a joyful kaleidoscopic dance routine.

'And she's in stilettos,' muttered Sophie.

'I didn't know you could play the piano,' said Mark as Joyce stepped off the keyboard and walked back to them. 'With feet or hands.'

'I'm a woman of many talents.'

'I don't think I want to know any more,' replied Mark.

'Get your mind out of the gutter. Right, we're going to get a drink. Mulled wine is all very festive, but I want a *real* drink.'

As they linked arms and walked away, Sophie turned to Mark. 'Your turn – what has been your most memorable Christmas meal?'

'A food question from Sophie, what a surprise.' He feigned deep thought with a finger resting on his lips. 'I know, Christmas S&M.'

'She said meal, you cretin.'

'It is a meal, Joyce dear: Christmas sausage and mash.' His cheeky little grin made it clear she had reacted just as he had hoped. 'Turkey and chestnut sausages – great big fat things they were with such a rich flavour – with parsnip and potato mash containing chopped bacon and mushrooms, topped off with a delectable red wine gravy, followed by a Christmas sticky toffee pudding. It was like a traditional sticky toffee pudding with added raisins and currants, lemon and orange peel, shaped like a Christmas pudding and served with a rich toffee sauce and lashings of brandy-infused custard. It was possibly the best meal of my life.'

They walked on in silence for a little while.

'Maze, anyone?' Mark asked as they neared the entrance.

'Why would you?' asked Joyce. 'Voluntarily getting yourself lost in the freezing cold, and fortunately, it's closed.'

Joyce was right. A barrier had been placed across the entrance as closing time approached, to give the staff plenty of time to rescue any lost visitors. Shrieks of laughter came from the far side as a group made their way out, and then it was quiet. It didn't appear that there would be anyone stranded tonight.

The maze pulsed with a glow of white lights that ran along the ground. Were they leading you to the centre or tricking you to a place of confusion? Bells jingled from time to time – were you being followed, or were you following?

'Oh, come on,' implored Mark, 'we're staff, we can break a rule or two. They're not going to lock up the gardens for a while yet. Come on, Joyce, or are you worried that we'll discover you have a dreadful sense of direction and you'll have to admit defeat and ask us for help getting you out?'

'I'll have to do no such thing.' She sighed. 'Alright, but you are buying the drinks when we finally get out.'

'Deal!' he declared.

Sophie laughed. 'Race you both,' she cried and vanished into the maze.

Mark held back and let Joyce go in first – he'd allow her to believe he was being chivalrous. She gave him a look of impatience, shook her head and glanced skywards before plunging into the murky gloom of the maze. Follow the lights or don't follow the lights, trust in them or your own instincts – that was the option offered to all of those who entered. Joyce would probably do her own thing. She wasn't a woman who took kindly to being told what to do.

Mark caught a final glimpse of shimmering blonde hair as Joyce turned a corner.

'Hope you're all behind me and you've not abandoned me,' cried Sophie from somewhere in the depths of the maze. 'If you're currently on the way to the Black Swan and I'm shouting at no one except the squirrels, then you're in my bad books, and I look like an idiot. Make that I *sound* like an idiot.'

'Any squirrels in the vicinity will have scarpered with all your bellowing.' Joyce's tone indicated that she had yet to buy into the spirit of things.

Sophie was on the far side, occasionally muttering, 'Oh drat... Bugger... Grrr... Yay! Oh no...' Giggles interspersed the narration of her journey.

'Oh, for heaven's sake...' came a strident exclamation.

'You alright, Joyce?' Mark called. 'Follow the sound of my voice.'

'No, follow mine,' added Sophie. 'I think I've got it.'

'I'm never going to follow either of you again,' was the rather stern response. For a moment, the lights vanished, and they were all plunged into darkness. Then a slow, dim pulse began. It was unnerving, as though a living, breathing creature inhabited the branches of the hedges, blurring the line between Christmas and Halloween, until the lights turned red and green and started dancing.

Mark paused, listening to footsteps, curses and giggles, and decided now was the time. He turned on his heels, remembered what he had been told about the fastest route to the centre of the maze and set off at a slow jog, trying to be as quiet as possible. He found himself ducking his head into his shoulders to remain out of sight, despite the fact that he wasn't tall enough to be seen over the top of the greenery.

Quickly finding himself at the centre, he took stock. Perfect. He had promised to pay the gardens team, who were working tonight, a case of beer. They had pulled out all the stops in the short time since the maze had closed to the visitors and had really earned it.

He sent Sophie a text message: *Ready.*

'Over here,' he heard Sophie shout. 'Joyce, this direction.'

'And that direction is…? I'm not eight feet tall. I am, however, extremely cold.' Mark laughed and quickly covered his mouth. 'Is that you I hear sniggering, Mark?'

'Never,' he said, still trying not to laugh. He couldn't help but grin to himself. He couldn't wait to see Joyce's face.

Footsteps were getting closer. Whose, he wasn't sure, and he held his breath, only letting it out when Sophie's head popped around the corner. Upon seeing everything set up, she smiled a smile that spread from ear to ear and could have lit up the gardens without the need of electricity.

'Come on, Joyce, where are you? It's dead easy.' Sophie leaned into Mark as she smothered her laughter. They could hear the heels of Joyce's shoes on the tarmac path as she approached.

'Do you really want to use the word *dead*…' Joyce burst into the centre of the maze, her coat a blaze of colour against the dark green of the hedge, her eyes wide and shoulders set back as though she was ready to let rip with her frustrations. But instead, there was silence and her mouth hung open.

Before her, a small table with three chairs took pride of place in the centre of the maze. It was covered with a silver cloth, tartan blankets hanging over the backs of the chairs. White candles made the table glow, and their light bounced off the champagne bucket that was the centrepiece. Sunk into the ice was a bottle of Moët & Chandon waiting to be opened.

'What the…'

'Language,' said Mark, interrupting Joyce's stuttered words.

'How did you…? When did you…?'

Mark pulled out a chair. 'Would madam like a seat? We have multiple blankets, hot water bottles, and about forty-five minutes, so get drinking, gal.'

Sophie lifted the bottle of champagne out of the ice. 'A glass of bubbly, madam? Accompanied by some delicious bite-sized lebkuchen, made by...' Mark coughed. 'OK, purchased by my own fair hands.' She started to pour as Joyce took a seat, taking the blanket offered by Mark and laying it across her lap. Mark prepared to place one round her shoulders, but Joyce batted him away.

'I'm not an invalid.'

With champagne poured and all three of them seated, blankets keeping them warm, Mark took hold of his glass.

'We thought you might like a little quiet celebration before the bedlam that is our usual family Christmas. Happy Christmas, Joyce, Sophie. Here's to friends.'

They raised their glasses, but before they could take a drink, Joyce added, 'I think you mean a-maze-ing friends.'

KEY TO A KILLER

CHAPTER 1

'I can't believe that we get to do this.'

Mark took hold of the staff pass that was hanging round his neck and waved it. 'Perks of the job, and in your case, of being related to a Charleton House tour guide. Come over here, we have a couple of Dickens first editions.'

The library at Charleton House was a bookworm's dream. It was all dark wood, large leather sofas and a collection of books to make the most ardent bibliophile exclaim in wonder. Mark watched as his guest walked slowly along the shelves, stopping occasionally to cautiously examine a spine. He paused next to a sliding ladder and glanced at Mark with a mischievous look in his eye.

'We could have some fun on this.'

Mark laughed. 'We'd need to oil it first.' His guest continued to examine the books, leaning forward to read the spines, his hands clasped behind his back as though he was forcing himself not to reach out.

'It's quite alright, you can touch them.'

Mark spun round and his companion jumped upright. An

elegant, regal-looking woman had entered the room and she smiled at the two men.

'Karl, this is the Duchess of Ravensbury,' said Mark. 'Your Grace, this is Karl Drinkwater, my cousin.'

The striking woman strode across the room and shook Karl's hand. Evelyn Fitzwilliam Scott, the 12th Duchess of Ravensbury, was a woman who exuded authority – tall, with perfect posture and sharp features that were softened by a gentle look in her eye.

'How lovely to meet a member of Mark's family. I can see the similarity.' Mark's height was matched by that of his cousin, although Karl was heavier set and didn't sport facial hair of any kind, let alone any that could compete with Mark's magnificent handlebar moustache. 'So, you're getting the tour.' The Duchess smiled warmly at Karl. 'Do you live locally?'

'No, Edinburgh. I'm here for a week.'

'Edinburgh is such a delightful city, a visit is long overdue. Speaking of which, that's a rather magnificent bowtie, Mark. Your family's tartan?'

'Yes, or at least I have distant links to the Robertson clan.' As he instinctively reached up to straighten the dark green, blue and red tie, Mark saw Karl contain a smirk. His cousin had teased him about it over breakfast, asking if it spun round or squirted water.

Karl turned, his eye caught by an object on a shelf. 'Is that a 1937 Imperial Number 1 typewriter, a Good Companion model?'

'It is, do you like typewriters?' said the Duchess, sounding impressed that Karl had identified it.

'Yes, it's what I do – I repair and restore them. That's a rather nice example, may I have a look?'

'Of course.' The Duchess removed it from the shelf and placed it on a large wooden desk next to a window that overlooked a courtyard. She turned on a beautiful Tiffany lamp to provide additional light.

'I don't think it's been used for decades, it's purely for display.

It will get dusted from time to time, but we haven't been looking after it, I'm afraid.'

'May I?' Karl's fingers hovered above the machine.

'Be my guest.'

Karl tried a few keys and the return bar. 'It needs some TLC and a thorough clean, but no more than that. I would be happy to take care of it for you.'

The Duchess rested a hand on Karl's arm. 'Would you? I would, of course, pay for your work.'

'And I wouldn't accept, Mark's tour is payment enough. I can probably do it before I head back to Scotland. Has it always been in the family?'

'Oh yes.' The Duchess was searching through a cupboard and pulling out the case. 'It does have rather a sad story behind it, I'm afraid.'

Mark could feel his heart beat a little faster. He loved a good story, and if it was about the Fitzwilliam-Scott family, then all the better.

'It belonged to a cousin of my father, James Grey-Lyons. He was tragically murdered when he was only twenty-five – on his birthday, in fact. I'm afraid the killer was never caught. This typewriter was in the room where he was murdered. He had just been presented with it, a gift from a friend who was badly injured in the attack.'

Karl had frozen with his hand resting on the typewriter. He pulled it away quickly as the Duchess finished speaking.

'Did it happen here?' he asked.

'No, no, at Berwick Hall, a few miles from here. James's family home.'

Mark knew the hall well. Like Charleton House, it was open to the public and he knew many of the staff. He had collaborated with a number of the Berwick Hall tour guides on joint projects, and although he knew that James Grey-Lyons had died young, he had not been aware of the circumstances.

'They kept that quiet,' he said, unsurprised that the Berwick staff had tried to keep the murder under wraps. Probably all too painful for the family.

'Yes, his mother was devastated, and as the years went by and the killing remained a mystery, she refused to discuss it. She didn't want her son's memory to be clouded by speculation and gossip, especially as it was so unusual.' The Duchess had found the case and lifted the typewriter carefully into it.

'In what way?' asked Mark, desperate to know more.

'When his body was found... please, sit down.' The Duchess led the two men to a couple of the large sofas before continuing. 'When the victims were found, the room in which they had been attacked was locked, from the inside, and the key was still in the lock. No one could understand how the killer had escaped.'

'A window?' suggested Mark.

'Yes, but it was shut and the catch secured firmly from the inside. There was no way someone could secure it from the outside.'

Mark doubted that, but kept his thoughts to himself. If you could break into a locked car with a coat hanger, then you could figure out how to secure the catch on a window of a historic house that was bound to be full of cracks from hundreds of years of wear and tear from nature.

'And his friend, didn't he see his attacker?'

'No, Mark, sadly not. Charles received a very severe blow to the head and was unconscious when found.'

The two men glanced at one another, intrigued.

'And you say this was a gift from one to the other?' Karl asked, looking at the typewriter on the other side of the room.

'Yes, James was quite a talented writer. He already had a typewriter, of course, but he had mentioned this particular model in passing to Charles, who then bought it as a gift. They were very close. Charles was devastated, as you can imagine, blamed himself for not being able to save James and later ended his own life. Then there was Sylvia, James's fiancée. She left the country and went to live in Italy. They had been a devoted couple. The whole thing was tragic.'

They all sat in silence for a few moments.

'Well, I really must be going. The Duke and I are having a high court judge for lunch.' She raised an eyebrow and Karl looked momentarily surprised that she would make such an obviously jocular gesture. 'Thank you, Karl, I do appreciate you looking at the typewriter for me. I'm not really sure what I will do with it, but I don't like the idea of it just sitting there, rusty and unloved.'

'I will do my best to return it to you as good as new.'

The two men stood as the Duchess left.

'So much for a holiday,' said Mark as Karl picked up the case.

'Give it a rest. I'll never forget the trip you made to Edinburgh last summer. After you learnt about the wizard who said the Devil had given him a magical staff, you spent the rest of the day doing research on him and you talked of nothing else all week.'

Mark grinned. 'Guilty as charged. Come on, I'll show you more of the house, and then I'll take you to the café. They have really good coffee.'

CHAPTER 2

'I think you've got some competition, Bill.' There was a teasing overtone to Karl's voice. 'You should have seen the way Mark looked at the Duchess, like a puppy dog.'

Mark's husband laughed. 'Oh don't worry, I know he'd ditch me for her in a heartbeat.'

'What are you on about?' Mark's attention was firmly on the laptop in front of him.

'Hey, get any closer to that and you'll get sucked in. You don't need glasses, do you?'

'I do not.' Mark sat back at Bill's comment, but his eyes didn't leave the screen.

'What's so important that you need to ignore our guest?'

'Karl isn't a guest, he's family. It's not the same. Well, it's not the same when it comes to him anyway, especially after he finished the last of the Tunnock's teacakes. They were meant to be a gift, but he emptied the packet.'

Karl laughed. He had brought the fluffy chocolate-covered biscuit and marshmallow treats with him from Edinburgh, knowing Mark loved them, but he also couldn't resist them.

Anyway, he had another packet secreted in his luggage and would surprise Mark with it later.

'I still want to know what's so important.' Bill rested a hand on Mark's shoulder and looked at the screen. 'Who is James Grey-Lyons?'

'Relative of the Duchess, he died in rather curious circumstances. The story had been relegated to the mists of time, but I've been able to find an old newspaper article that talks about it. It seems the family tried to cover it up and the details have been kept rather hazy – intentionally, I'm sure. I thought I'd give Ananya a call, she'll be able to tell me more.'

'She is?' asked Bill.

'Ananya Shah, a tour guide at Berwick Hall where it happened. She can show us the room as well – maybe we can work it out, solve the mystery.' Mark looked across at Karl who had sunk into a soft armchair with a glass of wine. 'Imagine that, you come south of the border and solve a murder that the Sassenachs couldn't figure out.'

'Whoa, wind the tape back, please.' Bill looked confused. 'Murder?'

Mark closed the laptop and poured himself a glass of wine with a dramatic flourish, allowing the liquid to trickle out of the bottle from a height. He then turned his chair to face the two men; he loved to tell a good story.

'If we're all comfortable, I shall begin…' Mark chose to ignore the roll of Bill's eyes.

CHAPTER 3

'It's always been something the family preferred not to talk about. They don't deny it happened and these days they're not going to great lengths to cover it up, it was just such an upsetting time that they don't discuss it.'

Ananya led Mark and Karl down a long gallery with a high ceiling and oriel and bay windows. 'This became the Earl's bedroom in the late 1600s, a smoking room in the 20th century and it's now used as a dining room by the current family from time to time. This...' Ananya had reached a wooden door at the far end of the room with a chair in front of it '...is now storage, having been a dressing room. During the period of time we're talking about, it became a sort of small sitting-room-cum-smoking-room that offered more privacy. It was a favourite of the men in the family. After 1958, when James died, the family didn't want it to be used for anything else, although they didn't go as far as turning it into a shrine.'

Ananya moved the chair aside and searched through a bunch of keys, eventually finding the one she was looking for.

'Apparently, James often met his friends in here, it was a sanctuary of sorts for him. He liked to come here to read and write, and I imagine it was very cosy, especially in the winter with the fire roaring away.'

The door opened with a loud creak. The group were faced with stacks of metal-framed chairs, their red velvet seats and backs indicating that they were used for events. The room felt cold. It was an unusual shape and most of the walls had been plastered and painted a pale blue-grey shade. A stone fireplace filled one corner, dust-covered boxes were stacked against the walls, and the small window was so dirty that the light struggled to find a way in.

'It doesn't look much, I know, but you have to imagine two big leather armchairs, a rug, the fire blazing away. There was a chest below the window, about the size of that one, but the original has long gone…' Ananya pointed to the right of the fireplace, '…and a small desk with a chair against that wall. I'm not sure about anything else. There might have been more furniture, but I doubt there was much.'

Mark stepped carefully around the stacks of chairs, trying to make sure that he didn't rub against anything and get dust on his outfit.

'I believe the police couldn't work out how the killer got in. May I?' He indicated towards the Tudor casement window.

'Go ahead. It will probably stick, but it does open.'

Mark pulled a silk handkerchief out of his waistcoat pocket and used it to protect his hand from the dust and dirt on the window catch. It was definitely stuck. He gave it a couple of shoves, then a final hard push and the window opened slowly and with some difficulty. He peered out, calling to the others over his shoulder.

'We're on the first floor, but someone could have climbed up. There's a drainpipe here and that climbing plant thingy looks pretty robust. The killer could have climbed that.'

Ananya shook her head. 'The gardens have changed since then. Plus the window was firmly closed and latched from the inside. That was the first thing the police noticed, after the door being locked from the inside. The key was still in the lock on this side.'

Mark pulled the window closed and started fiddling with the catch. Karl joined him and watched.

'What are you doing?'

'Trying to see if there is any way to manipulate the catch from outside. Some way you can lever it open and secure it again.' He ran his finger around the edge of the frame. There were no obvious holes or cracks. He closed the window and wiped his fingers on the handkerchief, folded it neatly and put it in his pocket. 'No, nothing.'

'What about the fireplace?' Karl walked over and tried to peer up the chimney.

'Too narrow,' said Ananya. 'I suppose a child might get down there.'

'Or Santa,' said Karl, his voice dampened by the dark hole as he examined it. 'Despite all the mince pies he eats, he somehow manages to get down every chimney. Now if there's a man who would be able to get away with murder, it would be him. He has the best reason in the world to break into everyone's house.' Karl stood up and grinned at Mark.

'I'll put it to the family,' said Ananya, smiling. 'You may have cracked the case. Why are you interested anyway? If you want to talk about it to the public, Mark, we really ought to speak to the family first.'

Mark shook his head. 'Nothing like that. Personal curiosity.'

'He wants to impress the boss,' said Karl.

'I have no doubt the Duchess would like to know what happened to her relative, but she wouldn't want me to go upsetting the rest of the family.'

'Then you should talk to Andrew Sales. He was a police officer at the time – young lad and his first dead body, apparently. He was in here the other week and I took his details. We're going to interview him for a memory project.'

Mark knew what Ananya was talking about, the conservation staff had done the same thing at Charleton House. People connected with the place were recorded talking about their memories, ensuring the history of the house and family remained for posterity.

'How about it?' Mark looked at his cousin. 'You up for a bit of sleuthing?'

Karl nodded. Now that he'd had a look at the scene of the crime, and how apparently impossible it was for someone to get in, his curiosity had been piqued.

'Let's go and see this Andrew bloke now. I'm only here for the week, the clock is ticking.'

CHAPTER 4

Retired police officer Andrew Sales was a large, jovial-looking man. Mark pictured him in uniform, the British bobby hat perched on his round head, rosy cheeked, calling small children scamps and sending them on their way after a paternal ticking off for being naughty. He and Karl were led into Andrew's back garden where they sat in the warmth of the afternoon sun under a large umbrella.

'Of course I remember the case, how could I forget it? Not only was it me first dead body, but it was one of the Grey-Lyons family and bloomin' weird too. We never solved it.' Andrew shook his head. 'What is it you want to know?'

'Everything,' said Karl eagerly. Andrew settled back into his chair and folded his arms.

'Alright then. Well, I was on patrol in Bakewell when the call came out. I was closest so I went straight to the house. All I knew was there had been a disturbance, so I wasn't ready for what I saw. I was led through the house to a small room by a funny little man, I don't remember his name. The house wasn't open to the public back then, so it was all quiet. I could see that the door had been forced open from yards away – there was splinters of wood all around and it had a big crack in it. I thought that was why I'd been called, someone had tried to break into the room.

'There was a young lad, worked in the gardens. He was outside the door, sat on a chair, looking very pale. I had quite the shock when I walked into the room. There was one chap sat in an armchair – looked like he was asleep, but he was at a bit of an odd angle – and another fella on the floor in front of the fireplace. I could see straight away that his head was a mess, the blood 'n stuff in his hair. I have to admit I was a bit shocked.

'It was the sound of the Countess running down the corridor shouting about her James that woke me out of it. The young gardener managed to shake himself from the state he'd been in and had the good sense to stop her entering. I was checking the fella in the armchair to see if there was a pulse when I heard moaning behind me. The other one, on the floor, he was coming around. It was clear that the one in the armchair – James Grey-Lyons – was dead, so I went to deal with... Charles. That was his name, Charles. Well, he'd had one hell of a bang on the head. I tried to make him comfortable until the ambulance took him off to hospital.'

Andrew stared off into the distance. Neither Mark nor Karl wanted to interrupt his thoughts. Mark's own mind was working furiously, trying to grasp at the significance of something Andrew had said. What was it?

Eventually, Andrew turned back to them and interrupted Mark's attempts to bring the elusive thread to the fore. Frustrated, Mark paid attention to what the elderly man was saying.

'I have to confess, I felt a bit useless. I'd not been in the force for long and I was still very green, and it being my first dead one, so I just waited until the DI turned up.'

'What did you think had happened?' Mark was keen to get Andrew's first impressions.

'Well, once I realised that the door had been broken down by the young gardener, I checked the lock on that. The key was still in it, on the inside, so no one had left that way. I looked at the window. The catch was firmly closed and it was only a small fireplace, so I couldn't imagine anyone getting in and out that way.'

Mark's mind cleared and the elusive thread came forward in all its glory. 'You say the gardener broke the door down,' he said eagerly to Andrew. 'Could he not have slipped the key back into the lock after doing that, and then made out that it had been there all along?'

'He could,' said Andrew, smiling wryly, 'had there not been half the household standing by to witness the act. He was a junior member of staff, so he wasn't going to be breaking no doors down before fetching the head gardener, the butler, the chief cook and bottle washer, Uncle Tom Cobley and all to give him the go ahead. And every single person – about ten of 'em in all – said the same thing. The window latch was secure and that key was in the door *before* it was broken down.'

Mark deflated. He'd been so sure he was on the right track. 'What about the murder weapon?' he asked.

'No idea! He'd been stabbed, James. It was clearly a very narrow blade, like *really* narrow. I wondered whether he felt it, to be honest. There wasn't much blood, just a little on his shirt. We couldn't find anything in the room that could have done that, so we had to assume the killer had taken the weapon with him. It must have been very distinctive.

'As for Charles, well, that was easier to work out. A stone had come loose from the fireplace, and it was lying next to him, with plenty of blood on it. The killer must have been surprised to find someone in the room with James and whacked him with it instinctively. James's death seemed to be very planned, so discovering the other man there must really have thrown him, or her.'

'What about a shard of glass, as the weapon used to kill James?' suggested Karl. 'That would be difficult to spot.'

'Or a corkscrew?' added Mark.

'We didn't find anything, although we scoured the place

multiple times. There was a corkscrew, but it wouldn't have matched the wound, and besides which, it had a cork on its end.' Andrew looked at them both with a thoughtful expression. 'So, why the interest?'

Mark and Karl glanced at one another.

'History,' said Mark after a moment's thought. 'Working out the puzzles of the past, and this is a real puzzle.'

Andrew nodded, apparently satisfied with the response. 'It would be grand if you worked it out. It might give Sylvia some peace too.'

'Sylvia?' Mark hadn't expected that. 'She's still alive?'

'She certainly is. Moved back over from Italy after her husband died.'

Mark's ears pricked up. 'She married someone else?' He exchanged a glance with Karl, who raised his eyebrows.

Andrew frowned. 'She did indeed, but don't go thinking there was any hanky-panky going on while James was still alive. It was a good two years later that she married an Italian chap. But now she lives Matlock way. She wanted to be near her children who all decided to live over here. Makes sense, she's getting on now.'

Mark wondered if there were other reasons, too: looking to the past; wanting to be close to James. A guilty conscience, maybe. Who knew, but it certainly wouldn't surprise him.

CHAPTER 5

Sylvia, Mark observed, was a small yet rather determined-looking old woman, with sharp clear eyes and a demeanour that left you with the belief that she knew what you were thinking, and had equally clear eyes in the back of her head. Sylvia's daughter had opened the door – the two men had phoned ahead and were expected. She'd led them to Sylvia's sitting room and left them with her mother, who had remained seated in a well-worn armchair as they entered.

'So, you want to talk about James, do you?' Sylvia sounded pleasant and welcoming, but Mark had decided that was just a way of disarming them. 'What do you want to know?' Beside her was a small table that seemed to hold all of her essentials: a book, glasses, tea cup and saucer, television guide, TV remote, a small diary and pen. If there was someone to bring her food, then she could sit there all day.

She looked at the two men intently, and Mark could see Karl shifting nervously in his seat. Mark had been concerned about quizzing an old lady about her murdered sweetheart, but not anymore. Sylvia looked like she could handle it.

'I... I mean we only found out about James's death a couple of days ago and we are intrigued, we'd like to know more. Everyone says it was impossible, and yet it happened. We want to find out how the impossible was achieved.'

'Many have tried and all have wasted their time,' said Sylvia. 'We kept the manner of his death quiet for as long as we could – we didn't want the attention it would no doubt have garnered, and we wanted to be left alone to grieve. The police investigation meant that a certain amount of information did start to leak out. Every now and again, someone crawls out of the woodwork and decides they know the answer.' She locked eyes with Mark as she said this. 'Of course, they never do. The way the killer carried out the act is as much of a mystery as *why* they did it.'

'I was going to ask about that, it might be a good place to start. Was there really no motive that you could think of?' Mark pulled out a notepad, his pen poised.

'No, none at all. James was the third of three sons, so he was unlikely to inherit the family wealth. He was a kind, sweet man who, as far as I know, never insulted anyone in his life. He was a writer, but he didn't pen anything that could be considered offensive. He didn't gamble, so he had no debts. Yes, he drank from time to time, but nothing that would cause concern, and I can say hand on heart that I believe he was utterly faithful to me. We were due to be married the following spring and we had never even seen a bump in the road, much less had to navigate one. So, as you can see, there was no motive that I can think of. I would say this was a senseless killing, but it occurred in his home in a locked room, not on a street corner, so that does not make an ounce of sense. Unless someone did it merely to see if they could.'

'What about Charles?' It was Karl's turn to ask a question. 'Could he have been the intended target?'

'We considered that,' Sylvia replied with a sigh of frustration. 'But no. Very few people knew he was there that night, and although he was a little more outspoken than James, he was well-respected and not a single enemy was identified. Certainly not one who felt so strongly that they wanted to kill him.'

There was something about Sylvia that Mark instinctively liked. She looked and sounded utterly fearsome, and spoke about the murder of her fiancé with a matter-of-factness that suggested she had spent a long time coming to terms with his death and was at some kind of peace with what had happened. She did not sound bitter or angry. Equally, she didn't seem to cling on to any hope that his killer would be found. Sylvia was a woman who did not carry hatred in her heart, she had taken control of her life.

Karl was now on the edge of his seat, listening intently. 'About Charles – we were told that he later died by suicide,' he said.

'Yes, it was so tragic. I don't think any of us were aware of just how hard the whole event had hit him. He was so concerned for everyone else. He was a great support to James's mother and he looked after me so well.' Sylvia smiled fondly. 'He even asked me to marry him, said James had asked him to take care of me if anything happened to him. It was so sweet of him, but he was only doing it to be kind. Handsome chap, Charles was always the one who attracted the ladies. In fact, when I first met the two of them, it was Charles, not James who caught my fancy.' The old lady's eyes twinkled for a second, then clouded with sadness again. 'But then I got to know James – gentle, kind James – and after that, I knew he was the man for me.

'Anyway, it was clear that Charles blamed himself for not being able to save James's life, despite the fact that he was unconscious and unable to help, especially as his father was a surgeon. Although Charles had not followed in his footsteps, he did have quite a lot of knowledge which, had he been conscious, might have been of use.

'We all hoped that he would eventually be able to move on. None of us blamed him. After all, there was nothing he could have done and he was very lucky to survive himself. Survivor's guilt, I believe that's what it's called. It was... oh, some two years after James died that I was told that Charles was gone too. He was close to his family, he had a lot of friends, he had me. There were so many people who could have helped, but he did a very good job of hiding just how much he was hurting.'

Sylvia was starting to slow down, and the two men didn't want to overstay their welcome. Mark glanced across at Karl, who took the hint and stood up.

'Thank you so much for your time.'

She started to call for her daughter, but Mark stopped her.

'It's quite alright, we'll find our own way out.'

They weren't quite at the door when Sylvia spoke.

'I didn't ask why you are interested in what happened sixty-five years ago and it probably won't make any difference. But if you are able to find out what happened, I would like to know.'

Mark promised they would tell her whatever they found out, and then the two men left the house, none the wiser than when they had entered it.

CHAPTER 6

'So, you've got the bug, eh?' Andrew laughed as he took Mark and Karl back out to his garden. 'I wondered if I'd see you both again. You've got that look in your eyes, like a dog with a bone. I take it you went to see Sylvia?'

'We did,' replied Mark. 'She is quite the woman.'

'She's that alright, marvellous, she is. Been through a lot, but she just stands up straight and keeps on going. Was she helpful?'

Mark looked thoughtful. 'I'm not sure. She didn't say anything particularly new, but it was helpful to get more of a picture of the two men and the circumstances.'

Andrew nodded. 'Always important, the character and the background, when you're looking at something like this. But I doubt you're here to discuss methodology, so what can I do for you?'

Mark glanced down at his notes. 'What else was in the room? Anything that could have helped the killer get in? Anything unusual?'

Andrew scratched his chin as he thought. 'There was nothing that stood out, and there wasn't a whole lot in there in the way of furniture or stuff. There were a couple of pictures on the walls, sketches of the building in gold frames. A wooden chest, but it wasn't big enough for anyone to hide in. I thought of that. The table was fairly simple…'

'Was it a table or a desk?' Mark interrupted.

'Table, one of those with fold-out leaves. It was against the wall with one leaf out. Do you think that makes a difference?'

'I doubt it. I can't see how, I just want to make sure we don't miss anything.' Andrew nodded thoughtfully. 'And the floor,' said Mark. 'I believe there was a rug on the wooden floorboards?'

'That's right.'

'Were any of the floorboards loose? Was there a way in from the room below?'

Andrew shook his head firmly. 'Not a chance, that building is solid as anything. It wasn't built as any kind of fortress, but the walls are right thick and the floors too. I don't even recall noticing a squeaking floorboard.'

Karl and Mark exchanged a quizzical look. They were both stumped.

'Did the men have anything on them?' asked Karl. 'Maybe they had something the killer wanted that would give us a clue, or he or she put something in one of the men's pocket to make it look like he had brought it in with him and it hadn't been used by the killer to gain access to the room.'

'My, my, I hadn't thought of that, no one did. Maybe you two should sign up with the Derbyshire Police. I can't be one hundred per cent sure because it was a while ago. James was wearing a shirt, no jacket. There wasn't anything in his trouser pockets that I remember, but then he was home and didn't need to carry anything around with him. It was different with Charles as he was visiting. He was smartly dressed, but his hat had rolled across the floor. I know he had a handkerchief because I noticed it had his initials sewn in. A wallet. He had a rather nice fountain pen that I have to admit I took a fancy to, but would likely cost a month's wages to the likes of me. The cork from the wine, and of course, he had brought the typewriter with him, but that was on the table ready to be used.'

'And no one was behaving oddly? No one had been spotted in the garden? Unusual visitors who could have secreted themselves away and everyone thought they had left?'

Andrew smiled at Mark. 'You really are thinking of everything, but no. Nothing unusual.'

After a minute or two's silence as they were all immersed in their thoughts, Karl spoke. 'I can't think of anything else. Maybe we should go back to Berwick Hall, Mark, take another look.' His cousin nodded.

'I was thinking the same thing. There must be something in there that can tell us what happened.'

'Well, good luck, lads. We couldn't find a single thing in there that could help us out, but if you can solve it, well, you deserve a medal, that's what I say.' Andrew stood up and shook their hands firmly before walking them to the garden gate. 'I imagine you'll bring a lot of peace to Sylvia as well if you work out what happened.'

CHAPTER 7

The two men sat in Karl's car reflecting on Andrew's words.

'I don't think he believes we can do it, do you?' Karl said, with amusement in his voice.

'Nope, not a chance. He reckons we're wasting our time, I'm sure of it, and maybe we are, but I do like the challenge.'

'It's like when I'm trying to work out what's stopping a typewriter from working. I've had a few where I just can't explain it and it's been a real head scratcher. The house could be on fire and I wouldn't notice, I get that caught up in it, but cracking it is the best feeling.'

'You're a nerd, do you know that?'

'Takes one to know one.'

Mark laughed. 'Touche. Back to Berwick Hall, then?'

'Yep, then we should go home. I want to do some more work on the typewriter, see if I can get it cleaned up for the Duchess before I go.'

'My instinct is it's something to do with the windows, so I want to take a closer look.' Mark was leading the way past members of the public who were examining the information boards in the Earl's Apartment. He nodded a greeting to some of the Berwick Hall staff who recognised him. 'Or maybe it was an inside job and the door lock had been fixed so that it could be unlocked with the key still in place on the inside.'

'Hmm.' Karl was deep in thought and nearly stumbled over a small child. 'The killer can't have hidden inside the room because there would have been a lot of activity and they would have been spotted if they had crawled out from under a floorboard. I know Andrew said the floorboards weren't an option, but he might have been wrong.'

'Perhaps, but if they could hide, they might have stayed there for a while, if they had supplies. They could have climbed out in the night and no one would be any the wiser. It would have been easy then for them to escape from the house.'

Ananya was waiting for them outside the heavy wooden door with the same large bunch of keys. She let them in with an amused look on her face; she knew how much of a blood hound Mark could become from her previous encounters with him. Karl immediately started knocking on the wooden panelling surrounding the door, the only panelled part of the room.

'You're wasting your time,' said Mark, coming over to him. 'Look, it's basically a screen. Unless the killer was no more than about four inches wide, or thin, or whatever, they couldn't have been in there.'

Karl grunted. He knew that from their last visit, but he was desperate for answers. Next, he moved aside a painting. It depicted a large, muscular angel with wings and a beard who was holding a baby at arm's length as if he didn't know what to do with it and wished it would stop crying. Karl tapped the wall – nothing. It was solid.

Mark lifted the lid of the chest.

'You'd be lucky if you could get both your boots in that, let alone the rest of you,' said Karl, peering over his shoulder.

'Can we move this?' Mark asked Ananya.

'Be my guest.'

The two men took an end of the chest each and lifted it away from the window. Mark bent down, trying not to kneel on the dusty floor for fear of spoiling his trousers, and started examining the floorboards.

'If the chest had a false bottom, someone could climb into it, then straight into a hole in the floor. The closed chest would hide any change to the wooden boards and the chances are that back then, the police wouldn't have done much more than open the lid and take a quick look for the murder weapon.'

Ananya looked amused.

After poking around the boards for any sign that they'd been tampered with, stamping on them to see if the sound changed and simply getting as close to them as possible and trying to see any inconsistencies, Mark stood slowly, groaning as he straightened up.

'Don't tell me you've reached that stage,' teased Karl.

'What stage?'

'The groaning when you stand up, sit down, lift something…'

'Sadly, yes, I'm an old man.'

'You're only six months older than me.'

'I know, so it won't be long and you'll be creaking too.'

Karl bent over and touched his toes with well-practised ease.

'Yoga. You should give it a go.'

'The killer would have needed to do more than yoga to get in a chest this size. You said the original was the same size as this?' Mark looked quizzically at Ananya, who nodded. 'There's nothing to indicate a hole below it in the floor and only a toddler could hide in this.'

'Maybe a toddler was the killer, convinced to carry out the murder on behalf of someone who offered them a year's supply of chocolate and a pair of roller-skates.' Surprisingly, Karl looked serious.

'You don't spend much time with children, do you?' Mark twisted one end of his moustache. He had another look at the catches on the window, but having given them a thorough going over the first time he and Karl had examined the room, he made a rather half-hearted attempt.

'I'm stumped, blooming stumped. The killer was some kind of magician.' He walked slowly to the door, followed by Karl and Ananya.

'I wouldn't feel too bad, Mark, you're not the first to be flummoxed. It seems that no one can figure it out. It will remain a mystery. Maybe it's better that way, the identity of the killer could cause a lot of heartache.'

'Maybe,' mumbled Mark, who was still deep in thought as he led the way out of the room.

CHAPTER 8

With the table cleared from their dinner of home-made lasagne and garlic bread, Bill laid out the marking he needed to do for the following day: piles of pupils' exercise books, some covered in bright stickers, some doodled all over, one or two carefully wrapped in paper to make a colourful cover of stripes or rainbows. Karl stationed himself at the opposite end, having placed the typewriter squarely in front of him on top of an old tea towel and laid a small number of tools out in a perfectly neat row.

'Are typewriter emergencies common? I assume they are if you travel with your tool kit,' teased Bill.

'Constantly, you'd be amazed. I'm always asked to attend the scene of a typewriter catastrophe when I'm on the road.' He glanced up at Bill and smiled. 'These aren't my usual tools, these are things Mark helped me gather up – a few pieces from a glasses repair kit, a screwdriver from a tool box in your garage that looks like it hasn't seen any action since 1982 or thereabouts. It depends how bad things are in here.' He peered into the typewriter with the torch on his phone. 'I might be able to sort it, otherwise I'll need to take it home.'

'And I'll have to come and fetch it on behalf of the Duchess, all expenses paid,' called Mark from the other side of the open doors that divided the house in two, the dining room on one side, the sitting room on the other. 'I could stay at the Balmoral Hotel, champagne served with every meal.'

'I'm going to guess that it's more likely you'll be sleeping in my spare room, if you can find the bed under all the clutter, and drinking cheap bottled beer from the supermarket up the road. The typewriter repair business doesn't lend itself to me having a wine cellar,' said Karl.

The two men at the table worked in silence, the sound of the TV in the background. There was a comfortable ease and peace about the evening. No one needed to speak; they were all engrossed in their work or entertainment, easy enough in one another's company that they didn't have to work at being together. Mark's attention had drifted from the TV programme and he was making notes, a spider graph appearing on the page of his notebook as he tried to link together everything he knew about the murder at Berwick Hall, and it wasn't much. In the end, the graph wasn't very web like.

Mark got up to pour a glass of wine for everyone. He leaned over Karl's shoulder as he placed them on the table.

'Does it work?'

'You can find out if you like. You got some paper?' Bill passed a couple of sheets across without looking up from his work. 'I still need a bit more time with it,' said Karl, 'and it needs a really good clean, but it should work OK. The keys will be a bit sticky and I doubt there'll be much or any ink on the ribbon, but we'll find out.' Karl stood up, wine glass in hand, and Mark took his place at the table. He fed the paper in, turning the knob carefully. After straightening the paper, he placed his fingers gently on the keys.

He felt a kind of reverence. This might have been the last thing that James had touched. Andrew hadn't mentioned there being a piece of paper in the machine, any typed final words, so perhaps Mark would be the first to use it since Charles purchased it for his friend. The joy of receiving this might have been the last thing the young man felt before being murdered.

Mark had no idea what to write. He couldn't think of any words worthy of a moment like this. The keys were smooth beneath his fingers and for a brief moment, he started to doubt whether he should type anything at all. Maybe he should let the final touch be that of James.

'Hang on, put the paper rest up.' Karl pressed a small button, then he pressed it again. 'I'll have to add this to my list of jobs, I need to…' He poked around at the back of the machine for a moment before a slim metal arm swung up behind the floppy piece of paper. It caught the paper awkwardly rather than supporting it squarely. 'Bugger, sorry. Hang on.' As Karl retrieved the paper, then made sure the rest was upright, he yelped. 'Ow! That's not right, may I take a closer look?'

Mark stood up and once again the two men changed places. Karl spun the typewriter around so the back of it was facing him.

'This has been altered. The arm should be a blunt, narrow, straight piece of metal with a rounded tip.' He sat in silence, until his cousin spoke from behind him.

'Are you thinking what I'm thinking?'

'I'd normally say *I hope not*, but on this occasion…'

'Karl, tell me if I'm losing my mind…'

'You're losing…'

'Shut up. Tell me if I'm wrong, but does that metal arm look like a blade? A very small, narrow blade that could fit the description of the type of weapon that might have killed James?'

CHAPTER 9

The leather sofa creaked as Karl made himself comfortable in the Charleton House library. He still couldn't quite believe that he was sitting down for coffee with a member of one of the country's most significant aristocratic families. Not only that, but the Duchess was pouring.

'I have to confess, I didn't think for one minute that you would solve the murder. I really thought you would just clean up the typewriter and return it to me, but then I should have known better.' She looked at Mark and smiled warmly. 'Your cousin has a marvellous ability to discover all sorts of wonders amongst our collections and stores.'

'You have a true treasure trove, Duchess, it makes my job extremely easy,' Mark replied, bathing in her compliment.

'So, I am dying to know what you discovered... sugar? Milk?'

'Oh, er, yes, just milk.' Now the Duchess was offering to add milk and sugar, Karl was staggered. 'Right, well, we, er... Mark, do you want to start?'

Mark, at ease in the company of the Duchess, sat back into the sofa with his cup of coffee in his hands.

'To be entirely honest, it was sheer chance. We checked every aspect of the room – the windows, door, floor and ceiling. It seemed impossible for anyone to get in from the outside, so everyone said it was an impossible murder. James dead, Charles injured and unconscious. No way in, no way out. There was nowhere anyone could hide.'

Mark stopped and took a sip of his coffee. He was enjoying telling the story, although it wasn't actually a story. It was a disturbing, sad and upsetting reality. Before he could continue, Karl, having found some confidence, stepped in.

'Charles and James had been close friends for a very long time. Charles had been an advocate of James's writing and expressed a keenness to support him. He surprised James with a typewriter he was particularly fond of for his birthday. A beautiful and thoughtful gift, I must say. I would be very happy if someone gave me one of those.' He eyed Mark and the Duchess laughed.

'You'd better make a note of that, Mark.'

'Charles arrived for the boys' night in, dressed as smartly as ever, and wearing a hat.' Mark had been nodding along as Karl spoke and now took over again. 'But Charles had an extra surprise, and not the pleasant kind that you would expect on your birthday. You see, he had tampered with the paper rest at the back of the typewriter and turned it into an extremely sharp little blade. It was only about 10cm long and less than 1cm wide. A blade like that is too small to get a good hold of, plus Charles would have ripped his hand to shreds trying, but he had planned ahead and brought with him a cork from a bottle of wine. The police did find a second cork in the room, but either got confused and forgot there was already one on the end of the corkscrew, or dismissed it as being from a previous occasion that Charles opened a bottle of wine. Either way they didn't view it as significant. With the blunt end of the blade inserted into the cork, Charles could get just enough purchase to stab his friend. Add to this the knowledge he had picked up from his surgeon father, and he would have known exactly where he needed to insert the blade in order to have the desired result – death.'

The Duchess shook her head slowly as she considered what she had been told.

'But what about Charles's injuries? He had been badly attacked.'

'It was self-inflicted,' said Karl. 'It would have taken a heck of a lot of determination, but he was able to give himself a bash on the back of the head. He was wearing a hat when he arrived at Berwick Hall, which would have hidden the injury, and once he had killed James, he hit himself with a stone that had come loose from the fireplace – or more likely, he had loosened it on a previous visit – to reopen the wound. Then he just had to lie down on the floor, pretend to be unconscious when the police entered, and then come round…' Karl made little air quotes as he said *come round* '…with some moaning and groaning, feign shock at the death of his friend and claim to have seen nothing, knowing that the chances of them finding the blade in the typewriter were remote, and he was right. It might be that he thought about trying to retrieve the typewriter, but felt it might draw attention to it.'

There was silence for a few moments as they all considered the circumstances that had been described. It had been cold-blooded murder, carried out by a man James considered a friend.

'But why?' asked the Duchess. 'From everything I've been told, they were each devoted to the other on an equal footing. They had been for many years.'

'Another devotion got caught up in the mix,' said Karl, getting carried away by telling the story as he poured himself more coffee, an amused Mark watching. 'James fell head over heels in love with Sylvia and fortunately, Charles appeared to approve of the match. He was perfectly happy for Sylvia to spend a lot of time with him and James, and there was no sign of Charles feeling like a gooseberry and getting annoyed at the new situation. In reality, despite having no trouble attracting female attention with his good looks, Charles was also very much in love with Sylvia. The bottom line is he wanted her for himself. It must have been excruciating for him to watch Sylvia and James's relationship blossom, when all the while he was falling further and further in love with her, believing that he would never be able to have her.

'Eventually he concluded that he had to have her no matter what and took action. Once James had died and, I presume, he believed an appropriate amount of time had passed, Charles proposed to Sylvia himself, couching it as being about taking care of her and something that James would have wanted. Sylvia thought he was just being thoughtful and looking out for the fiancée of his best friend, but marrying her had actually been his intention all along. She turned him down.

'When she went on to marry an Italian man, Charles was devastated. He had killed his dearest friend for nothing, and so in a fit of remorse, or maybe despair, he killed himself. The dates fit – Sylvia's marriage and Charles's suicide happened within weeks of each other – so we're sure this is the reason behind the crime.'

Silence descended once again while they all considered the events of the past. A large clock gave a low, rumbling, masculine chime, the perfect sound for the room, but none of them registered it.

Eventually, the Duchess spoke softly.

'Have you told Sylvia?'

'No,' answered Mark. 'I didn't feel that we were the right people to do that.'

'I'll do it,' she replied without hesitation. 'I know her a little – enough that, along with my family connection to James, it wouldn't seem strange for me to visit and break the news to her.' She looked at the two men intently. 'You are sure that was what happened? It does make sense, but if I am about to tell an elderly woman that a friend she loved and trusted killed her fiancé, then I need to be sure.'

Mark and Karl glanced at each other. They were absolutely certain.

'The police haven't confirmed it one way or the other. When we gave Joe the typewriter, he said it would be handed to some kind of cold-case team. He was convinced by our theory, but it's not official, not yet.'

'Well, perhaps I can couch it as preparing her for the likely outcome, not wanting her to be shocked if it comes to light that Charles was indeed the killer. Sylvia is a very strong woman, but she was heartbroken when James died. I was once told by another cousin that Luca was never her true love. He was a good man and they were very happy, but James was the only man she ever really loved.'

EPILOGUE

'So, I'm related to a celebrity. Will you still acknowledge me when we're out in public?'

Mark laughed. He'd just finished telling his cousin about his latest project, a ten-minute slot on a weekly TV news programme where he would be talking about local history.

'For now, but I might have to reconsider if I get my own series. You can carry my bags.'

Mark had his feet up after a long day of delivering tours at Charleton House. His bright orange socks stood out like little traffic cones against the dark fabric of the sofa, his orange tie had been loosened and hung skew-whiff around his neck. A phone was wedged between his ear and the sofa.

'Well, I have my own celebrity news,' declared Karl. 'Some of my typewriters are going to be starring in a new World War Two film. It's set at that training college for spies that was based at Arisaig House in Inverness-shire. I'm providing three in total. It's a nice little sideline I'm developing, supplying period typewriters to film and TV companies. I don't know why I didn't think about it before.'

Mark could hear the sound of a bottle being opened. 'You on the cheap supermarket beer?'

'No, celebrating with some locally brewed stuff. A gift from a happy customer.'

'Speaking of which, a happy customer is what I'm calling about. The Duchess was very pleased with the typewriter you sent down, she couldn't tell the difference between yours and the Good Companion that Charles gave James.'

'Any idea what the police are planning to do with the original?'

'Not a clue. Even Joe doesn't know, but he doesn't work in that department, he just handed it over.' Mark swirled the red wine in his glass.

'What good is a brother-in-law in the police if he's not going to give you inside information?' Karl's tone made it clear he was joking. He'd met Joe many times and liked him. 'What's the Duchess planning for it, then?'

Mark thought back to the meeting he'd had with the Duchess the previous week. 'A small display in the library, so it won't be seen by general visitors, just those on special tours where we'll talk specifically about James's writing. It's more of a prop for us to use as a talking point than a display that people will look at on their own. We're not going to discuss his death, but she wants to make sure that his writing is enjoyed by a much wider audience. The typewriter will be paired with a photograph of him and a few examples of his work. She'd like to publish a book of his essays and poems, but that's a bigger piece of work and only in the very early planning stages.'

'You should tell her that if she ever gets James's typewriter back, I'll happily continue to work on it.'

'You won't find handling it rather gruesome, especially the blade itself?' Mark waited for a response while Karl took a drink of beer. He could hear loud gulps.

'Nah. It doesn't look gory, it's just a typewriter that needs cleaning and a new paper rest fitting. It happens to have a rather fascinating story behind it, and we both love a good story, don't we.'

Mark smiled and took a sip of wine.

'We certainly do.'

THE LETTER OF THE LAW

Detective Constable Joe Greene brought his motorcycle to a stop outside a smart semi-detached house and removed his helmet. Leaning against the garden wall was a rather scruffy-looking man; his t-shirt advertised a beer festival that had taken place fifteen years ago, and it stretched over a belly which provided further evidence of the owner's love of the calorific 'bread in a glass'. Curly hair flopped over his ears and hung in his eyes.

'Alright, Father. Sorry I'm late,' said Joe as he climbed off the bike.

'No worries. Figured I'd wait for you out here so she doesn't have to repeat herself.'

'Lead on. When we're done, we can go and have a pint.' Joe had technically clocked off from work, but when a call had come through to the station that Father Craig Mortimer, an occasional drinking buddy of his, wanted a chat, he was happy to agree to meet him on the way home.

'Is she very upset?' asked Joe as they approached the door.

'She was earlier; she might have calmed down by now. I'm not surprised, though, it's a horrible thing to have happen and she doesn't deserve it.' Craig knocked on the door before pushing it open. 'Jean, it's Father Craig. Can we come in?'

A friendly looking woman with dark hair containing a few streaks of grey, a red cardigan over her shoulders and drying her hands on a towel, appeared at the end of the hall. She looked to be somewhere in her sixties.

'Of course. You must be the police,' she said as she looked over Craig's shoulder at Joe. 'Oh, off duty?'

'Just, yes. Detective Constable Joe Greene, nice to meet you. I'm on my way home – excuse my appearance.' Joe ran his fingers through his hair as though that would improve things and make up for his ancient bike kit. He wished he hadn't chosen to wear his oldest, most severely scuffed and oil-stained leather trousers to ride to work. The jacket was bearable, if you ignored the way the colour had faded unevenly over the years. 'I'll just take my boots off.'

'There's no need. So long as they're not caked in mud, you're fine, really. I've put the kettle on.'

Jean led them into her sitting room, then left them there while she answered the summons of the whistling kettle. It was a comfortable space; the furniture was quite old and well used, but looked welcoming rather than tatty.

After Jean had returned from making the tea and poured them both a cup, Joe asked to see the letter.

'It was delivered by hand this morning. I was out shopping and it was waiting for me when I got back.' The letter, which had been made by cutting words out of a newspaper, was short and to the point, describing Jean as an overweight old woman whom nobody liked. It also said she was a dreadful minister and should resign. Joe examined the letter and its envelope. The latter was self-sealing, so there wouldn't be any DNA on it.

Looking up, Joe could see tears welling in Jean's eyes. 'You have no idea who is behind this?' She shook her head.

'Jean is incredibly hard-working,' Craig explained. 'She's done a huge amount for the churches under her watch. She's very well thought of by everyone who works with her. This just doesn't make any sense.' He turned to Jean. 'You're the last person I would expect to be getting hate mail.'

She smiled weakly at him.

'And outside the church?' Joe asked between bites of a Jammy Dodger. He was ready for his dinner, but a couple of biscuits would tide him over. Jean shook her head.

Joe looked at the letter again. He hated to admit it, but no crime had been committed at this point.

'Is there anyone at all you can think of who might have reason to be … frustrated with you?' He was trying to keep his language subtle; he didn't think *'Have you annoyed anyone to the point of hate mail?'* would be helpful. Jean was quiet for a moment, then looked at Joe; she seemed hesitant to speak.

'Well, there is the lad next door. His parents are away and he's been playing his music very loud. I went to talk to him, ask him to turn it down, that was yesterday afternoon.'

'How did he react?'

'As you'd expect from a sixteen-year-old boy. He grunted and told me where to go, in none too delicate tones.'

Joe and Craig looked at one another. This was a valid route to explore.

'I'll have a chat with our young music lover, but I'm afraid at this stage it's all I can do. Let's hope it's a one-off and they've got things off their chest, but please, call me or Craig if you get anything else.'

Jean smiled. 'Thank you, detective. To be honest, it's just a relief to know that I have people on my side who will take this seriously. I've never really minded living on my own, I'm used to it now, but it's hard at times like this. You're both very kind.'

. . .

Craig had gone on ahead to the pub to get the drinks in, but Joe had hung back, knocking on the door of the house next to Jean's. He knocked again, then a third time. It was six o'clock and he found it hard to imagine that even the laziest of teenagers would be in bed at this time. He couldn't hear any music, though.

Eventually the door opened and a tall, gangly youth with heavy eyebrows glared at him. The smell of stale takeaway food wafted out of the door.

'Yeah?'

Joe introduced himself. 'I believe that the lady next door has had a word with you about the volume of your music.'

The lad rolled his eyes. 'I turned it down, alright? I can't turn it down any more, I won't be able to hear it, miserable old...'

'Alright, none of that. Were you keen to get your own back?'

The teenager looked at him blankly. 'Whaddya mean? She doesn't play music, not that I can hear. How can I tell her to turn it down?'

'I didn't mean that. Did you drop a letter through her door? Maybe in a moment of anger?'

'What letter? Why would I do that? I don't understand.' The boy really didn't, Joe was sure. This lad would probably have cursed at Jean, thought he was tough to do so, but Joe doubted he would even have thought of cutting out words to compose the spiteful letter he'd seen. In fact, Joe wasn't sure he knew how to read and write. No, that was unfair, but still, Joe's instinct told him the boy didn't have it in him.

'If it turns out you're in the midst of a bout of amnesia, just stop it, alright?'

'I told you, I didn't do anything.'

Joe attempted to give him the look of a worldly elder, and then walked off. It was time for that pint.

. . .

Craig had found them a table in the corner of the Black Swan, a pub that belonged either in a cosy TV murder mystery or on a Christmas card, with its open fire and big wooden ceiling beams. Craig didn't look anything like a member of the clergy, but everyone knew who he was and it had taken him ten minutes to get from the bar to the table as at least half of the pub regulars wanted to stop him and say hello. Working at Charleton House, a glorious display of baroque opulence that had been standing for over 500 years, Craig was responsible for the chapel within the magnificent building. What had once been a private place of worship for the Duke and Duchess of Ravensbury and their family was now open to the local community, and Craig was kept busy.

Joe sat down next to him and Craig slid a glass over.

'One pint of faux beer. You could always leave your bike here and crash at mine for the night.'

'Thanks, but I'll pass. Next time.' Joe glugged down half the amber liquid and sat back. 'I needed that.'

'Long day?'

'Aren't they all?'

'Yeah, I've noticed that,' said Craig. 'The days seem longer as I get older, and at the same time, they go by quicker, and before I know it, I'm at the end of the month and behind on everything.'

'Age, mate, and I don't think God can stop that happening. He might have a place saved for you upstairs, but down here, you're getting on in years.'

Craig grimaced and nodded.

After a conversation about the recent winning streak of Craig's favourite local football team, The She Devils, a squad of women who were sponsored by the Black Swan and known for not taking prisoners, they moved on to the reason for their get-together.

'So, what do you think?' asked Craig.

'About the letter? Let's just hope that's the end of it, that whoever sent it wants to make a point, and they've moved on. It's probably some sad bugger who spends their evenings shouting at the TV and they'll be distracted by something else come the morning. It would be nice to send a message to them, though, stop them doing it altogether, but it's never that simple. Do you know Jean well?'

Craig shook his head. 'We met at an annual conference and kept in touch when we realised how close we live to one another, but I've never had any reason to go to St Luke's parish.'

'She has a good reputation?'

'Stellar, but not a goody two shoes, know what I mean?'

Joe did; he hadn't detected any kind of sickly-sweet, too-good-to-be-true essence about Jean.

He quickly emptied his glass. 'I should get going, I promised Ellie I'd take her for a curry and I'm already late.'

'When am I going to hear wedding bells?' asked Craig. 'I'm assuming I'll get asked to do the deed.'

'Give us a chance, it's not much over a year.'

'We all thought you'd end up with Sophie from the café up at the house, but Ellie seems like a nice lass.'

'She is, and who's "we"?'

'Everyone. All of us. Each and every one of us who has ever spent time in a room with the two of you.'

'Nah, she's more like a sister is Sophie. I did think about it, but after a while, it got a bit weird. We're still good friends, though.'

'Glad to hear it, she can do the catering for the wedding.' Craig grinned and Joe punched him on the shoulder.

'Let me know if Jean hears any more,' Joe called as he walked away.

Joe didn't have to wait long. Only two days had passed before another letter was hand delivered to Jean, accompanied that evening by a phone call with nothing but silence on the other end. The letter made it clear what the sender thought about female ministers and compared her to Satan.

Joe knew that it was now a case of harassment. It didn't take him long to find out that the call had come from a pay-as-you-go phone, the SIM card bought locally. He was convinced this was the work of someone with a vendetta.

He sat across from Jean in her kitchen, this time in a smart suit and officially on duty. Joe had a boyish look to him and there was little that showed signs of ageing, something he found useful when talking to witnesses. Those who concluded he was young and inexperienced often found themselves saying more than they intended to, so not always being taken seriously could have its advantages. On this occasion, even though Jean was the one Joe was trying to help, she revealed some things that he suspected she'd rather have kept to herself.

'My contract at St Luke's is coming to an end,' she explained. 'I had a three-year contract and it's now up for renewal. I had thought that it would be smooth sailing, but at the last parochial church council meeting, two of the churchwardens withdrew their support for me. One of them, Frank Porter, was particularly vociferous. He claimed that I was difficult to work with and not a team player. I was so surprised, he hadn't complained before. It was an open meeting so a lot of people heard. I was mortified.'

Joe could tell that the criticism had stung and it still upset her all these weeks later. He passed her a tissue from a box on the coffee table. While she blew her nose, a black and white cat rubbed itself against his leg, leaving a layer of fur on his smart trousers.

'You held on to the post, though?'

'Oh yes, it was only the two who voted against me. Frank resigned, though.' She looked up at Joe; they seemed to be thinking the same thing.

. . .

'So, when is the sting operation?'

Joe, who had made a visit to Craig in his vestry at Charleton House, looked confused.

'What sting?'

'You know, lie in wait in an unmarked van around the corner from Frank's house on bin day, then when he puts his recycling out, you dash round, scoop it up and go through the paper and find the newspapers with all the words missing.'

'That would certainly add an air – a pretty pungent air – of sneakiness to our investigation, but it would also be illegal. I need a warrant to go through his stuff and we haven't got enough evidence for that. Plus, he might not be much of a recycler, he doesn't sound like the kind of bloke who'd give a stuff about the environment.'

'So, what are you going to do?'

'Not a lot at this stage, I'm afraid. I'm really hoping it's going to tail off into nothing and Jean will be left in peace.'

'You said that last time, look what happened.' Craig had a point, but he knew Joe's hands were tied, so he changed the subject. 'You coming to the pub quiz tomorrow? The Black Swan has just started it up. Course, a load of staff from here have formed teams and they're all history buffs and have PhDs and the like, so you'll need to be a member of Mensa to stand a chance.'

'I wouldn't be much use, then.'

'Can't disagree with you, but you could bring Mark. If he's married into the family, you may as well make use of him.' Mark, Joe's brother-in-law, was a tour guide at Charleton House and his brain was like a sponge for historical facts, absorbing odds and ends that would be of no use anywhere other than a pub quiz.

'I'll ask. In the meantime, you need to improve the quality of your coffee, or I'll be arresting you for attempting to poison a police officer.'

'Keep complaining about the refreshments I serve,' Craig said with an exaggerated air of mystery to his voice, 'and you might find it's more than just an attempt.'

The following evening, Mark was filling in their pub quiz team form while Craig updated Joe on what was happening with Jean.

'She had another one this morning. Same style of lettering, same self-sealing envelope. Called her a Satan worshipper and compared her sexual habits to Mary Magdalene, which makes him look like rather an idiot and not as devout as he likes to make out 'cos nowhere in the bible does it suggest she was a prostitute.'

'She's lucky that he hasn't threatened to mess with her food.' Mark was still scribbling as he spoke. Joe and Craig remained silent; they knew he'd get to the point in a moment. 'Abraham Lincoln received rather a lot of hate mail – I suppose people in positions of power do – and one of his threatened to put a spider in his dumpling.' There was another pause. 'I once received hate mail.' He looked up. 'Okay, I'm ready. When are they going to get this show on the road?' He linked his fingers together and stretched his arms out in front of him as though he was preparing for physical exertion.

'Go on, then,' Craig encouraged him, 'you can't stop there. Tell us about the hate mail, unless it's too difficult to talk about.' He rested his hand on Mark's shoulder and displayed an expression of concern that held a hint of mockery.

'Oh, that. It was from an ex-boyfriend; he hoped that I would be killed by kittens with laser eyes.'

'You poor thing,' said Craig, with definite mockery in his voice. 'I'll go and get us another round of drinks, I think you need something for the obvious lingering shock.'

After losing the quiz by one point, because none of them could be sure of the names of all the Spice Girls and their last-ditch guess of Flirty Spice was received with loud and prolonged laughter from much of the room, the three men settled down for a final drink before heading home.

'So, what do you make of this Jean woman?' Mark asked. 'Is she likely to get someone's back up to such an extent that they'd rather spend the night cutting up newspapers than enjoying a good book?'

'Let's put it this way,' replied Craig. 'I spoke to another member of the PCC committee, after Joe had told me what had happened with Frank, and it seems that when Jean's appointment was put to a vote at an open meeting, dozens of the congregation turned up to show their support. She is hugely popular, so no, I don't think she is.'

'Poor woman,' Mark muttered, shaking his head.

'I know, but there's not a lot else we can do at this point.' Joe was genuinely disappointed. He hated the idea of Jean suffering as much as the others did, but whoever had it in for her knew what they were doing.

Over the next couple of months, the letters kept coming; every week or so, another would arrive, the contents getting more and more personal. Forensic test results always came back blank.

Then there were the silent calls, all from the same mobile phone. Now they were coming in the early hours of the morning, so Jean was both upset and utterly exhausted, but she refused to ignore the phone for fear that it was one of her congregation who needed her. Both Craig and Joe made a point of checking in on her, making sure she was okay and trying to deal with the fact that amongst the church community, there was a building resentment towards the police for their lack of progress. Joe was always dreading the next call to say there had been another letter, or worse, and he was as frustrated as anyone. He enjoyed Jean's company; her unexpected love of motor racing was something he shared and it gave them plenty to talk about each time he popped round.

The dreaded next call came when he was on a night shift. It was 3 am on a Thursday when he drove over. The lights were on throughout the house and a little white car was parked on Jean's driveway. He was let into the house by a woman who looked about 120 if she was a day, and she was furious.

'Right, young man, this is getting ridiculous. What are you going to do about it? That's what I want to know.'

'It's alright, Betty, let him through. He's doing his best.' Jean's shout was followed up by a loud sniff and Joe found her sitting on the sofa, being comforted by another woman who looked only a year or two younger than the gatekeeper who had opened the door to him.

'This is Betty and Marion; they were kind enough to stay over for the night and listen out for the phone so I could get some sleep without missing any possible calls from someone who genuinely needs me. I'm afraid I woke when one of the calls came through.'

'That was my fault,' said Betty, looking a little sheepish. 'I had this with me.' She held up a whistle. 'Wanted to deafen the bugger, only I blew it a bit hard down the phone and woke Jean. Sorry, love.'

'Oh, you're alright, I like the idea of you bursting his eardrums. Well, I came down, and… well, he called again straight away. He's just not stopping.'

'Couldn't believe it,' said Marion. 'Barely minutes had gone by and he was at it again. The whistle hadn't put him off, it seems nothing does.'

Joe looked at the three women before him. He was slightly afraid of them; he just wished that Jean's harasser was too.

. . .

Joe wheeled his chair from one side of the office to the other and brought it to a halt next to the desk of Detective Sergeant Colette Harnby, who was trying to dab a coffee stain off her jacket with a look of annoyance. Joe had just got off the phone after a call from Jean. He looked frazzled, and his hair, which needed a brush at the best of times, was definitely out of control. DS Harnby opted not to say anything about his hair; she realised from the look on his face it wouldn't go down well, which was saying something about a man who was so mild mannered.

'D'ya reckon we could get CCTV installed outside Jean's?'

'We'd need a very good reason – has something else happened?'

'It has.' He sighed. 'She got a parcel delivered this morning, by hand. It contained dog sh… I mean dog excrement. Distressing enough as that is, it also means that they're still comfortable enough to make a visit to her house and don't plan on slowing down. If anything, things are ramping up.'

Permission was granted.

It was two days later that there seemed to be a ray of hope. Another letter had arrived, once again with a self-adhesive stamp and self-sealing envelope. As Joe stood before Harnby's desk reading it out to her, he found it hard to hide the excited grin that kept trying to push its way onto his face.

'*…and you're not a team player…* recognise it?'

'Not offhand and you better tell me quick. I'm afraid you're going to leave a puddle on the floor at this rate.'

'Those are carbon copies of the words that Frank used at the open meeting. We've got him – this gives me a solid reason to bring him in.'

Harnby smiled; she looked as relieved as he felt.

'Go on, get the warrant, and we'll search his house. It's about time we had some good news.'

Joe grabbed his jacket and practically skipped out of the room.

The search of Frank's house found nothing. He did read the same newspaper that had been used to form the words of the letters, but his copies were intact. And anyway, with a readership of over 300,000 across the UK, his daily paper alone was hardly going to stand up in court as evidence of his guilt.

He looked concerned as he was interviewed.

'I don't like Jean, I never have and I make no secret of it. We've butted heads since the day she joined us. I've done my best not to rock the boat, but I had to speak out when it came to the continuation of her contract. I don't believe I'm the only one who feels this way, so it was important the matter was brought to a vote. All this is public knowledge.'

'So you deny sending the letters.'

'Of course I do. It's a blooming stupid thing to do, and as for late-night phone calls, I haven't got the time or energy. It's childish; well, it would be if it didn't cause so much distress, and I don't want to cause that. I've always used the official channels available to me.'

He had a point; he'd been open and honest about his feelings from the very beginning. Joe's heart was sinking when he was faced by Frank's calm self-assurance; he knew the man was innocent, which left him precisely nowhere.

A week later, the police removed the CCTV that had been installed. There was nothing on the tape of any use, and Jean and her OAP bodyguards had been updating their community on the current state of affairs, including telling them that there was a camera positioned outside the house, so there was no point keeping it there. But, in the hope that they would also update their friends and associates about its removal, Joe had replaced it with a covert camera and not said a word.

Joe lived in a converted chicken barn at the end of his parents' garden. The small stone building was upside down; you entered into a double bedroom with an en-suite shower room, and then climbed an ornate iron spiral staircase to get to the lounge-cum-kitchen. The Tardis-like building was surprisingly light and airy and gave him the best of both worlds; the privacy of his own place, with his parents' kitchen and utility room only a hundred yards away. Some weeks, his own kitchen wasn't used at all, his mother taking pity on him and leaving him a plate of dinner in his fridge (and if she was in a particularly generous mood, she'd take his laundry with her, although she always insisted he come and collect it so she could try to wheedle any local gossip out of him).

Joe had his feet up and was watching clips of old TT races on his laptop, a mug of tea and a half-eaten packet of Hobnobs next to him, when Jean called him. He didn't mind being disturbed on his day off; he wasn't up to much. Jean was clearly distraught and, when he'd managed to calm her down, she told him the disturbing news that she'd received a delivery; a dreadful, upsetting delivery which made Joe so angry, he wanted to punch something. The parcel contained a dead gerbil, and a note informing Jean that she was soon to be just as dead.

Joe called Craig and asked him to go round to Jean's. He then called the station, asking for an officer to be dispatched to collect the animal. From one perspective, this rather macabre delivery was good news.

A short while later, two officers were sitting in front of a computer screen at the police station. DS Harnby hadn't minded Joe coming in on his day off, either, she was just annoyed that he hadn't brought coffee and pastries from somewhere more interesting than the station canteen. His inability to juggle coffee on a motorbike was, in her opinion, a weak argument.

Once he'd promised to go and fetch snacks after they'd done, he pulled up the footage from the covert camera. Jean had been pretty clear on the period of time that the parcel must have been dropped off on her doorstep because she'd gone out shopping between 10am and 1pm and it had been waiting for her on her return. Joe was hunched over, staring at the screen. He and Harnby watched the three hours of footage on fast-forward, pausing it from time to time, then they went over it again. Jean's front door was blocked by a large bush, but the entry to her driveway was clear and gave them a great view of any comings and goings.

'Get any closer and you're going to get sucked in.' Harnby grabbed Joe's shoulder and pulled him back into his seat. 'I can't see.'

They watched in silence. After watching and rewatching, forwarding and rewinding, they had to admit it was clear no one had walked down that driveway. Not the postman, not a paperboy; not even a neighbourhood cat.

Neither of them wanted to be the first to speak, putting what they now knew into words. Joe pulled on his coat and together they walked to the station car park. This was going to be the strangest and most uncomfortable couple of hours he had ever experienced.

Craig and Mark stared at Joe with open mouths.

'It was Jean all along? She sent all those things to herself?' Mark said with incredulity in his voice.

Craig looked baffled. 'I don't know what to think. I don't know if I should be as mad as hell or upset at how she played me… us. What did she say?'

'Nothing. She didn't say a word, not at first,' Joe replied. He thought back to the smile and look of relief on Jean's face as she had opened the front door, which had turned to confusion, and then an expression devoid of emotion as she spotted the impeccably dressed and stern-faced DS Harnby, and the uniformed officer standing behind her. As they searched Jean's house, they had found, tucked in a desk drawer, newspapers which had been cut up, words missing. A simple, inexpensive mobile phone was in another drawer, and Joe would have staked a lot of money on it being the phone that was used to call her landline. That, he realised, meant that when the supportive old women had stayed over, Jean had been calling the landline from upstairs. When another call had come through as the three of them stood by the phone, she had likely pressed redial on the mobile in her dressing-gown pocket.

He didn't like to think about where she had got the gerbil from.

Once they were back at the station and her solicitor had arrived, Jean started to speak, but only to say that if she were them, she'd be thinking the same thing; that she'd done it all herself. Later, she repeatedly said that the whole thing stank; that whoever had set her up had done a brilliant job.

The three men took long drinks from their pint glasses.

'Was she lonely?' asked Mark as he wiped foam from his moustache.

'No, she was very busy with the parish, always planning or attending events. Everyone… well, most people liked her,' Craig explained, and then turned to Joe. 'Have you any idea why she did it?'

'Nope, and we might never find out.'

'What will she be charged with?'

'It could be wasting police time, maybe perverting the course of justice. She'll certainly have her day in court.'

Craig nodded sadly and, after taking another drink from his glass, said, 'Well, I'm glad it's all over, but that's the only positive thing I can find in all of this. Mark, you look deep in thought.'

Mark nodded. 'I've just remembered. A couple of years ago, I got some nasty letters. I'd got the chance to work with an archaeologist at Charleton House, but he tried to blackmail me.' He sounded deadly serious.

'Why? What happened?' asked Joe.

Mark glanced up at his two friends, then replied, 'It turned out he had a lot of dirt on me.'

There was a long pause, then Joe and Craig gave a simultaneous groan.

'After that,' said Joe, rolling his eyes at his brother-in-law, 'the next round is on you.'

DEAR MONTY: A CHRISTMAS LETTER

Dear Monty,

As this is your first Christmas, I feel duty bound to pass on the benefit of my own experience and knowledge, which are both considerable. I am aware that you are living in the house of a police detective. I am familiar with this person and although I have found him to be very generous with his attention towards me, his job is to look out for anyone not playing by the rules, so *your* job might be harder for you than many others, living as you do in his home.

I must warn you that despite being a lot of fun, Christmas is very hard work and takes real commitment if you are to carry out all your duties. You should not be deceived by all the bright lights, aromas of turkey or sounds of bells; there is work to be done. However, you are young. You have the opportunity to establish some rules and traditions of your own. It is also important to pace yourself and take lots of naps. If you are lucky, there will be a log fire in front of which you can sleep.

Let's start with the Christmas tree: this is fundamentally a climbing frame of the highest quality. At your age, this activity will be viewed as 'cute'. Make the most of this. Next year, he might not be quite so keen and might even try to find ways to prevent you reaching the tree entirely. You must not, however, let anything he does deter you, but we can discuss this further next Christmas when it is more likely to be an issue.

Also, the tree is basically decorated with toys, so don't let anyone or anything tell you otherwise. It is your job to do everything you can to knock them off, and then play with them. Expect photographs to be taken of you at this point, especially when you are in the coloured glow of the tree lights, which I am led to believe makes a particularly good picture. (Get used to this, you will have to adjust to having a camera thrust at you on a regular basis during the festive season. This is actually a sign that you are doing your job well and are suitably 'adorable'.)

In our profession, we are provided with a particular source of joy at this time of year in the form of tinsel and other garlands. My oh my, will you have some fun! These can be pulled off the Christmas tree, swung from (I suggest leaping off the furniture in order to reach them), dragged through the house and wrapped around ankles. I mentioned bells earlier; there will be a lot of bells. It is your job to determine where the sound is coming from, identify the bell and then play with it. This is particularly important if it is attached to someone's hat.

Your human might try to wrap you in a string of lights for a photograph. This is exactly the kind of situation that your claws were made for. You cannot allow him to humiliate you in this way. If he humiliates you, he humiliates us all. The same response is necessary if he tries to put a seasonal hat of some kind on you (as you can probably tell, it is advisable to ensure you have sharpened your claws prior to the festive season). If he attempts to put you in a Christmas jumper, which is not common but not unheard of either, again, claws.

On Christmas morning, if you are concerned that he or any of his guests have overslept, then locate yourself outside of the relevant bedroom and begin to retch, as loudly as possible. For some reason, this wakes humans far faster than even their alarm clock. They also appear particularly alert on these occasions. This is a useful skill to have beyond Christmas. If you have not been fed breakfast, retch. If you are not being given enough attention, retch. The mere sound will get you all the attention you desire.

Presents under the tree look far more exciting than they actually are. If you find you have a spare moment, then it can be entertaining to spend a little time climbing them (they provide excellent access into tricky Christmas trees). Equally, you can give them a good chew. However, they rarely smell particularly interesting and once opened, they are typically of very little interest. Humans will expect you to play with the wrapping paper once the presents have been opened; they seem to think this activity is cute. For some reason, they don't feel the same way about morning newspapers. It's confusing and I have no explanation.

Whilst we are on the subject of gifts, I do not believe it is necessary for us to give our humans a gift, our presence in their lives is more than sufficient. I did once try and it was not gratefully received (apparently, a fresh pigeon is not deemed a suitable present, even if delivered to the recipient in bed). As a result, I swore that never again would I make a special effort on Christmas Day.

A great deal of food will be consumed by the humans at this time of year and it presents us with many opportunities. Everyone is extremely busy, particularly in the kitchen, and so it is easy for them to lose track of what food they've left where. This is where you benefit: it is not uncommon for meat-based products to be left unguarded on the kitchen counter, so practise finding ways to reach this surface in advance of it happening. Guests at parties do not pay attention to their food either – they are too busy trying to juggle their drink and plate and engage in conversation all at the same time, so sneaking a piece of cheese is easy to do in this scenario. Alternatively, use your cuteness to your advantage around visitors. They are unlikely to know the rules of the house and will simply give you food.

You mentioned something about a dog who will be in attendance on Christmas Day. Remember, dogs are fundamentally stupid creatures. They can be trained to do tricks, and any animal who spins around for a measly little treat is a certifiable lunatic. A golden retriever is known to be particularly soft and gullible; it is almost guaranteed that he *will* be in a Christmas sweater, which, as well as making him look stupid, reduces any false sense of superiority that he may possess.

That said, I advise that the two of you consider teaming up. In order to reach food placed on high surfaces, you can climb up onto his back. I also suggest that you make yourself as adorable as possible by napping under his ear and playing with his tail. These sorts of activities are likely to get you both a lot more treats.

Monty, I hope this advice will be of some use to you. I realise it is a lot for a kitten to take in and there are bound to be setbacks, but when that happens, have a quick nap, followed by a good stretch, a lick of your paws, and a scratch of the side of the sofa. Then you'll be ready to start all over again. But don't forget the most important part of all of this: have fun! Oh yes, and vomit at least once on the good rug. There is no particular reason for this, other than it is one of the core tasks of any self-respecting cat, and it being Christmas doesn't change that.

I must end this letter here. My own human has returned, and I have to run to greet her at the door – she is *extremely* needy. Please give me a meow if you have any questions.

Happy Christmas,
From
Pumpkin.

THE SKELETONS OF STONE COURT

Joyce Brocklehurst
2 Larkspur Close
Derbyshire

Dear Kenneth,

I hope this finds you clasping a martini and admiring the latest addition to your art collection. I, on the other hand, am in my rather draughty office with thousands – well it sounds like thousands – of schoolchildren fighting over erasers and chocolate in the shop outside my door. If they don't simmer down I will have to go and read the riot act.

Many thanks for the photograph of Mother. I remember that dress well, it's a Mary Quant. My sister kept hold of it after Mother died, they were a similar size. I must see if I have a photograph of Bunny wearing it.

No, Kenneth dear, I have not had tea with the Duchess recently. I manage the shops, not her bedchamber. She does like to discuss my plans for the retail offer and she's very involved with the local designers and suppliers whose work I sell, but she has yet to step on my toes. Year on year, profit continues to rise, so I think she's aware that I know what I'm doing.

We have a new member of staff who started a couple of months ago and would amuse you on a sartorial level. Mark – the latest to join the ranks of the tour guides – is so thin, he'd have to run around in the shower to get wet. Dresses like some sort of dishevelled throwback: a waistcoat that's too big for him, handkerchief poking out of his pocket that really needs tidying up – it looks like he's just blown his nose on it rather than artistically tucked it into place. His shoes are rather nice but <u>very</u> worn – second-hand, I imagine. I can see the kind of look he is going for, but he really needs to focus on the detail. Probably spends most of his time with his head in a book. You would love to be his wardrobe mentor, I'm sure. I must give him the details of a tailor I know in Manchester, who will be able to create a rather fabulous fitted waistcoat.

Mark seems to think that he's witty, which he might be in some circumstances, but he tries too hard in my opinion. I swear he breathes through his ears because he never stops talking long enough to draw in air. He's overly excited by some repair work that needs to be done in my office. There is a large project to replace much of the ancient pipework around the building and some of that is taking place in a small courtyard on the other side of my wall. The work will involve digging up the floor at the rear of my room and you should have heard the response from some of my supervisory staff when I told them what was happening and that I'd have to temporarily relocate myself to a desk in the office they share.

No, Kenneth, they were not up in arms at the idea of me working in the same space as them, and don't deny that was the first witticism that came to your mind. Well, alright, that might have been part of it, but their main concern was, to quote them, 'disturbing the ghost'. I feel ridiculous just writing that and yes, you read correctly. A number of them are convinced my office is haunted. It used to be their workspace, but it got to the point where they refused to enter. They complained of pictures falling from the walls overnight and when they arrived for work, they would discover them broken on the floor. The same thing happened to me, but I eventually accepted fate and didn't bother rehanging them.

That ghosts are involved is ridiculous, of course. The walls are uneven and you have to be very careful when putting anything up. We also have a particular member of the team who is a bit of a joker and it's not beyond the wit of one or two of our security guards to have a little fun on their night-time patrols. But at least my staff don't bother me when I'm working in here.

Of course, you are no doubt thinking that the ghost is too afraid of me to make an appearance, which is as it should be. It would get short shrift if it decided to start ooooh'ing into my ear, especially if I was in the midst of writing my reports and I ended up recording the wrong figures in error! No being, corporeal or otherwise, would be so stupid.

Anyway, the point is that I now have a disturbingly large proportion of my team distracted from their work as they prepare for a mass haunting once the floor is dug up. I really don't have the time for it. Ghosts or no ghosts, we have a busy summer season to prepare for... hang on...

...I had to go and tell those blasted children to keep it down. Their teachers were doing their own shopping out of sight of their charges. You would have assumed they were both deaf, the way they were ignoring the racket. Of course, I gave them what for about their responsibilities and as I return to this letter, there is nothing but a low hum of voices from the other side of the door. Perhaps I missed my calling and I should have been a teacher. Perhaps not. I'd probably murder the little buggers.

Well, my dear Kenneth, thank you again for the photograph, it was very thoughtful of you. I must return to my work or, in your mind, hobnobbing with the landed gentry. Feel free to picture that, it's far more glamorous than the reality.

Best wishes,

Joyce x

From the Desk of the Duchess of Ravensbury
Charleton House

Dear Annabelle,

I'm not sure if this will arrive before you leave for Paris.

I have some rather macabre news. Building work in Stone Court – you know, the little one round the back of the main shop – revealed a gory discovery: two skeletons, apparently adult males! Can you imagine? I'm not particularly squeamish, but it was rather a shock.

Do you remember Joyce Brocklehurst, the Head of Retail (how can you forget her? She dresses rather like an explosion in a paint shop)? Your father grumbles about her, but I think there is a grudging respect. He's never been one to suffer fools and it's clear she is of a similar mind – perhaps they are too alike. At any rate, she is certainly an interesting character: an older woman determined to plough her own path in life.

Anyway, back to the story. Joyce was telling us that a number of her staff refuse to spend time in her office, which backs onto the courtyard where the skeletons were discovered. They believe it is haunted. Joyce isn't at all fazed by the situation, but the news has spread like wildfire among the staff and various rumours are being passed around. One is that the two men died as the result of a duel, but I have heard of no such thing occurring here. Duels yes, resulting deaths, no. Another is that they were German prisoners of war who were trying to escape and were found hiding on the estate. Quite why they would be buried in that location, I have no idea. Competing suitors for the hand of an ancestor, thieves who were caught red-handed and were dealt justice rather swiftly – the list of possible stories behind the skeletons goes on. However, I don't recall any tales that could be related doing the rounds when I was growing up, so we are currently in the dark. I do hope we are able to give them names and we will, of course, provide a decent reburial, regardless of what we are able to find out. I promise to keep you posted.

Actually, we have a new tour guide who is very excited about the find and has asked permission to help try to discover more about the two men. As long as it doesn't impact on his job, I don't mind. He's a very charming young man, although his dress sense is as interesting as Joyce's, and he's fascinated by history… which could be why he wears a pocket watch!

I am increasingly concerned about your younger brother. Oliver does have a wayward streak in him and I fear that it will lead to trouble. Last weekend, he drove his Land Rover into a ditch, destroying a wall in the process, whilst racing one of his friends. He was brought home by the police who recognised him and decided not to press charges. We don't encourage that sort of favouritism, of course, but I can't say I wasn't grateful. He takes after your father – until I came along and he changed his ways. I'm joking – he remains a bit of a Jack the lad and I wouldn't have it any other way.

Anyway, back to the point. When you next see Oliver, I was wondering if you could have a bit of a big sisterly word with him. He really needs to think about some kind of career. He certainly needs to think about channelling his energy into less risky activities and he won't listen to your father and me. Do have a chat with him if the occasion arises, I would be ever so grateful.

Edward appears to have settled well into New York life. I must confess that I do rather hope, once this current contract comes to an end, he will decide to return and find a job in our area. He will not struggle as an architect around here and he really ought to spend some time in Derbyshire as the future Duke. It would be helpful for him to start building relationships with the local community.

Thank you for humouring your mother with handwritten

missives. As useful as emails are, they don't have the charm of letters. I doubt I would have enjoyed reading the correspondence of previous generations in the archives half as much if it consisted of emails that had been printed off.

Right, I must go and badger your father to write a letter to Edward. He will complain and tell me they spoke on the phone only last week, but once he has settled next to the fire, I have poured him a glass of whisky and handed him his favourite pen, he will secretly enjoy it. He's a romantic at heart.

Take care, my darling, enjoy Paris.

With love,

Mother xxx

From the Desk of the Duke of Ravensbury
Charleton House

Dear Edward,

Your mother has insisted that I put pen to paper and write you a 'proper' letter, and who am I to argue? I already know that New York is treating you well and I am beginning to get the impression that you would like to remain there a little longer. Of course, we'd rather you were back home in England, but you'll have your hands full once Charleton House is yours, so enjoy yourself.

Talking of having one's hands full, we have finally commenced the project to replace all the major services: pipework, cabling, lighting, and we're upgrading all the fire safety systems. Costs an absolute fortune and we'll be on fundraising overdrive, especially in light of the five-year building-improvement plan that we're keeping our fingers crossed the trustees will approve. I'm rather hoping that you'll host a couple of dinners for us when you're here in the summer. I'm sure you can talk some of our wealthier guests into handing over large cheques.

The current building work has resulted in a rather fascinating, and somewhat macabre, discovery in Stone Court, which I seem to recall was one of your favourite hide-and-seek places when you were small. Two skeletons were unearthed during the pipework replacement in that area. It caused quite a fuss, as you can probably imagine. All sorts of rumours abound and the office next to the courtyard is believed to be haunted.

Bearing in mind that the Head of Retail Joyce Brocklehurst works there, I'm hardly surprised that some of her staff feel unnerved in the place. The woman could make a stone cry. Your mother says I am overly harsh and that she is doing wonders with our shops. She also says that if I spent some time with Joyce, I would warm to her. I'm not so sure. Between you and me, the woman bloody terrifies me.

Anyway, back to the tale at hand. It has been confirmed that the two skeletons are male, both somewhere in their twenties when they died, and date from the seventeenth century. There was quite a bit of damage, almost as if they had been beaten or had something dropped on them from a great height, and numerous bones broken. We were informed that the position the bodies were found in indicated that they had been buried in a hurry. There was also evidence of lime, pointing towards an attempt to hasten decomposition. Needless to say, it does rather look as though foul play was involved, but further investigation is required to determine exactly how they died.

Murder is clearly the hot topic of the day, but I have never heard of anything happening here. We have had numerous deaths at Charleton, but not a single murder to my knowledge. Of course, this discovery might change all of that. Might they be family members? I find it very unlikely. Our family is full of so many characters and fascinating stories that I know I have yet to hear all the tales, but surely one involving murder would float to the top very quickly. There may well be a distant relative or two who vanished or were believed to have moved abroad, and then nothing more was heard of them. Perhaps there was a disagreement that resulted in the unfortunate demise of the two souls in the courtyard, but there would need to be a third who then took the secret to their grave.

I was chatting to a rather pleasant new member of staff, a tour guide who is very keen to delve into this whole business. He's rather green, so I don't know if anything will come of it, but he certainly has the enthusiasm. Even if he just gets things moving and then we pass the research on to a more established member of staff, it will be a step in the right direction.

In the meantime, I will catch up with one or two members of the family to see if anyone recalls stories about vanishing relatives – or even staff, for that matter. I wonder what further building work will dig up. I have no doubt there are many, many other metaphorical skeletons in the closet, or courtyard, that we are currently entirely unaware of. You will eventually inherit those too! Go and enjoy the Big Apple, or whatever it is they call it, while you can.

By the way, your mother wants another dog. Heaven help me.

Take care of yourself,

Father

Mark Boxer
14 Valentine Road
Bishops Church
Derbyshire

Greetings, my fine friend,

I hope it‚s a braw day up in Edinburgh and you‚re not feeling peelie-wally. Pour yoursel' a wee dram, take a seat on your bahookie and wheesht while I tell you my news. See, I‚m fluent!

Are you impressed that I*;M*I'm am writing this on the typewriter you bought me for my birthday in the dim and distant past? Guilt got the better of me and I decided it was high time that I gave it a go. My initial thoughts…… it's bloody hard work. I assume it gets easier, and quicker ? !

So, what can I tell you? I;m not much of a letter writer, but if I acn write as much as I can talk (I do have some level of self-awareness), then I should have a magnum opusby lumchtime.

I think I'm settling into the new job well. I still can't believe that I'm working at Charleton House, of all places. This is THE place I have wanted to work for as lo ng as I canremember, and I know it so well that learning all the facts for my first tours wasn't very difficult at all. I just had to le arn what order they wanted them to be delivered in. Everyone has been very nice, the othet guides have been very welcoming, and I‚ve already met both the Duke a d ~~Duchess~~ the Duchess

I will be stuck with the daily public tours for a wh ile yet, but I already know I want the chance to deliver VIP tours, and come up with my own. What's amazing, though, is that after just a couple of months, I found myself doing some research in the hallowed ground that is the muniment room. That's 'the archives' to the common man. Pour yourself a dri n k and get ready for this.

So, there is some repair work going on, andduring excavation there was a rather grim discovery...... Two skeletons wree found!!! They are male, dating from the seventeenth century. There is some damage to the bones, which indictaed that it might have been foul play.

I was told by Joyce – the head of retail or retail manager – something like that – her staff thinkher office, which backs on to the courtyard where the skeletons were found, is haunted. She disagrees, but I'm not surprised. No ghost in its right mind would make an appearance when she is around, or at least if it did, she would send it packing, making sure it bought some souvenirs on the way out. Amazing woman, tough as old boots – or at least, that's how she comes across. Got a hair-do that would make Marie Antoinette proud, and Joyce has probably had a few people guillotined in her time as well. She is generally mocked (behind her back, no one is brave enough to say anything to her face) for her wardrobe, but she really knows what she is doing. When we first met, she was head to toe in fuchsia and I wondered if I'd stumbld across a previously undiscovered subspeciees of flamingo. On closer inspection, I realisded how magnificent the outfit was. Mind you, she talked to me as though she was the duchess and I a mere underling. I doubt we're going to become friends any time soon.

On the other hajnd, I thought you and I were friends, Karl. My finger tips are going to start bleeeding any minute. Are you sure typewriters weren,t first invented as an instrument of torture?

Where was I? Oh yes, so, this discovery has set tongues wagging, but no one knew of any murders that had taken place at Charleton House. Neither the Duke nor Duchess could recall any stories being told by relatives and they couldn't find any references in diaries or letterws written by the Duke's ancestors when they had a cursory look. They also asked family members, but were drawing a blank. So, I decided to take a chance and ask if I could look in the archives to try and find out more. I got the impression that the Duke didn't take me that seriously and was humouring me until the curators could get round to doing it, but I was determined to show him what I could do.

And how did I do? Brilliantly, of course. I dug around in the archives looking for significant events in the 1600s. The biggest thing was the rebuilding of a large portion of the house. It was a massive piece of work and late in 1687, an enormous wall collapsed, injuring eleven workers and killing two. The head carpenter was given the job of providing a decent burial and money to make the arrangementsx– I found reference to it in financial records from the time. It seems that he pocketed the money instead and found a quiet , hidden part of the house to bury their bodies. He would have covered them in quicklime in an attempt to destroy the evidence (of course, we now know that it actualljy delays decomposition).

We can be pretty sure this is what occurred as the carpenter did a similar thing on another job site a few years later, only that time he was caught as he attempted to bury the bodies. It might have been beginner,s luck that I found the clues and put them together so quickly, but I;ve certainly made a good impression on my new employers.

So, is Joyce's office haunted? I will leave that for you to decide.

How do you do this? I swear I am going to lose my finger nails and there are a monumental number of errors, it looks like a 4 year old has been banging away at the keys. I think I've also got RSI. You know I like avoiding too much to do with the modern age, but typewriters should come with a health warning. Not that I don't love it, on displayon a shelf! If you ever get another letter from me, it will be written with a fountain pen. Just saying!

Take care,

Mark

DEAR MONTY: AN UPDATE

Dear Monty,

Thank you so much for your note updating me with regards to your first Christmas, it does sound like a successful debut festive season. I am sorry that the Christmas tree fell over as you climbed it. However, I wish to reassure you that you are not to blame, and it was a risk that perhaps I should have warned you about. It only occurred because your humans bought an inferior quality tree. Perhaps they will choose more wisely next time.

I am very pleased you instinctively knew to go into cuteness overdrive following the incident: gaining eye contact, rubbing your face against your human's chin, burying your head in his neck, and then curling up to sleep in his lap were all wise actions, and I have huge hope for your development into a very fine feline. You do, however, still have a great deal to learn, and now that Christmas is over, I feel that it is important to share more of my knowledge with you.

I find it advisable to eat all and any food presented to you. You have no idea what mishap may befall your human and how it might affect the services they provide for you. If you have a built-in supply of nutrients (it is not 'fat' as I have overheard some people most rudely saying), then your chances of survival will increase greatly. Quite frankly, it can be a matter of life and death. I have been called podgy, plump, portly, corpulent, but I think of myself as voluptuous and curvy. One particular visitor to the house called me a 'lard-arse'. I stuck my paw in his drink when he wasn't looking.

If a human makes a noise which is intended to be a meow, respond in a similar tone. Continue this for as long as possible. I have had hours of fun this way. They will think you are conversing with them, while you can be greatly entertained by the gibberish they are producing. The bonus is that they think you are a genius – which we cats are, of course, but for many reasons other than the one they think.

If you are taken to the vet (something to be avoided if at all possible), scream loudly and continuously. If you are lucky, a neighbour will come over, believing that you are being catnapped. Even if they cannot prevent the visit taking place, there is a very strong chance that the sounds of your screams will inhabit their soul and they will sneak you treats from this point onwards.

Speaking of neighbours, please remember that you are not beholden to any one person. I have two others who feed me. I simply walk into their respective homes, and they welcome me. It might take multiple attempts until you find a human who receives you in this way, but they are out there. Don't give up.

Wake your human at least once during the night; you need to check that your supplier of food is still alive. They will be flattered by your apparent inability to go for one sleep cycle without displaying your love for them (or, at least, that is what we let them believe). Techniques that I find successful include sitting on their chest and staring at them until they feel your presence and wake. The shock they will exhibit stems from the joy they are experiencing at the sight of you. If they sleep on their front, sit between their shoulder blades and paw their back continuously.

Alternatively, you can try purring loudly whilst walking back and forth over them. One technique I highly recommend is extending your claws slightly and tapping them on the face until they wake. This has a particularly high success rate for me. I know of some cats who will simply sit on their human's face, but I find this to be rather an uncouth practice and don't endorse it.

When your human is using their phone or computer, do all you can to disturb them. First of all, that is valuable time during which they should be focused on showering you with attention. You are also assisting them with cutting down on something called 'screen time'. They should not have too much of it, it is not good for them. Walk on the keyboard of the computer, lie across one of their hands (the one they appear to use the most). Rub your face against the phone hard enough to knock it out of their grip. They will be persistent in their use of these items; you must persist in return.

If you find yourself sitting next to an object whilst on a table or shelf, it is your job as a feline to knock that object onto the floor. The humans have various theories as to why we do this: boredom, attention seeking, practising our hunting skills (although I have yet to find a mouse that just sits next to me, waiting to be eaten). I do it for the very simple reason that I like watching things break, it amuses me.

Not all our feline friends enjoy the human lap. I, however, think it's a marvellous place for a nap. It is also the case that many humans gain a great deal of pleasure from this, which manifests in something called feline paralysis. The result of this is that they are unable to move for some time, so you are guaranteed a good hour or two of sleep.

I have a suggestion for a marvellous way to occupy yourself in the warmer months, which I assure you, young Monty, are on their way: stealing items from washing lines. You can up the stakes by stealing things from baskets while the owner's back is turned (the tension is higher, but the reward equally so). I'm currently up to 14 socks, 3 pairs of knickers and a bra, which I am particularly proud of as it was a challenge to pull that through the hedge. They are currently hidden under the shed. They won't be discovered as my human has not been near the shed since she moved into this house – she's not exactly 'green-fingered', as I believe the humans call their inexplicable predilection for growing plants.

Two final things for you to remember before I bring this letter to a close:

If a human strokes or scratches your belly, there is only one acceptable response. You must make them bleed.

You have a right to absolutely everything. Repeat it to yourself: "I am a cat, therefore everything I see is mine."

Do update me on your progress in a few months.

Your friend,

Pumpkin.

A PRIVATE MURDER

CHAPTER 1

'I want to show you something.' Mark pointed to a painting above a door frame. 'This depicts the Flaying of Marsyas, a satyr or nature spirit who challenged the god Apollo to a musical contest. It was painted in the early 1700s. Marsyas is the one tied to a tree with his right hand above his head. Now, look closely. Can you see anything out of place?'

Sophie and her mum, Christine, peered at the painting, concentration etched on their faces.

'Hmmm, give me a minute,' said Christine, stepping forward, even though that wouldn't improve the view. 'I'm not sure, but it does feel like something isn't right. Do you see it, Sophie?'

'I already know what it is.' Sophie worked at Charleton House and had been through this door hundreds of times, often hearing the assistants pointing out the interesting feature of the painting to the paying visitors.

'Wait a minute. The watch, he's wearing a watch!' Christine looked rather pleased with herself. 'Well I never, how on earth did that happen? The early 1700s, you said? But that can't be possible.'

Mark gave an amused little bob of his eyebrows.

'Well done, yes. The right wrist of Marsyas. Where there should be a rope binding is actually a wristwatch. The theory is that it's a joke added by a cheeky restorer in the 1950s.'

'Very cheeky,' agreed Christine. 'Did he get in trouble, or has his handiwork remained an open secret ever since?'

'It's unlikely he was found out at the time, otherwise he would have been instructed to fix it.'

'I rather like it,' said Sophie as the three of them walked away. 'I know he should never have done it, but it's just another piece of history, another story attached to the place, a lovely quirky one.'

'Sophie, you're condoning vandalism,' mocked Christine. Then the three started to laugh about the additions they would make to some of the other paintings.

The rarefied air of the ornate baroque rooms they were wandering through was tainted by the crackle of a radio on Mark's belt. He stepped aside and had a brief conversation over the airwaves before returning to them.

'My group is here, I'm giving a tour to some octogenarians who will probably be more interested in where the café is than anything I have to tell them.'

'What's wrong with that?' Sophie, who was the manager of all the cafés at the house, laughed. She looked at her watch. 'Shame they'll all be closed now.'

'We did tell them that when they booked, but this was the only time they could do. No doubt they'll still complain. Christine, a delight as ever.' Mark gave an old-fashioned little bow and strode away.

'You know he's shown me that picture before,' said Christine once Mark was out of earshot.

'He's shown it to me more times than I can count, no matter how often I've mentioned that I know all about the wristwatch. You'd think he painted it. Maybe he did.'

Christine laughed. 'I'm not sure I can see him at the top of a ladder defacing part of the art collection. He certainly has the sense of humour to add something like that, though.'

They walked through a few more rooms in silence. Christine had visited the house many times when Sophie was a child. They had explored it and the gardens as a family, Sophie always wanting to know what was hidden behind doors marked 'Private', before dragging her parents to the café (the key way they had managed to get her to visit historic houses in the beginning was a promise of cake).

Now, Sophie worked there. Who would have thought that bribing her with cake could have led to a job like this? Christine took great pride in telling her friends that Sophie worked at Charleton House and spoke regularly with the Duke and Duchess of Ravensbury. She had yet to meet them herself and was rather hoping to avoid an encounter with them as she had no idea what she would say.

As they passed the staff in each room, they would get a formal smile or nod of the head. Some knew Sophie well enough to pass the time of day, others were just being polite to someone who had a staff pass hanging from the lanyard around their neck. Christine felt that some of the staff were different, though, not quite as friendly as they had been in the past.

Something was definitely not right in the big house.

'I see what you mean about the mood,' she said to Sophie. 'There is an air of watchfulness and nervousness. They're certainly not themselves.'

Sophie had told her mum about the thefts of paintings that had happened recently. Three had been taken so far, and all from under the watchful eyes of the assistants who stood within the routes, talking to the visitors about the history of the house and providing a layer of security. The paintings had all been small; not so small that they would have fitted in someone's handbag, but small enough that with a bit of ingenuity, they could have been smuggled out. There had been changes: a couple of extra staff had been recruited, security guards did additional patrols, visitors were not allowed to bring in bags larger than a compact handbag, and a marquee had been erected near the entrance to operate as a left luggage facility.

'I'm surprised that all the paintings below a certain size haven't been removed,' said Christine, as she looked at a small portrait of a boy with his dog. The boy held a chicken under his arm and the dog looked as if he wanted it for dinner.

'The Duke and Duchess are adamant that the actions of one won't spoil the pleasure of many, especially now that extra precautions have been taken.'

'Still a bit of a risk though, isn't it?'

'Yes, and the head of security has gained a lot of grey hair over the last couple of weeks. Based on his pained expression most days, he's probably developing an ulcer too.'

A tall, stern-looking visitor assistant nodded at them as they approached.

'Hello, Rick, how are you?'

'Well, thank you, Sophie.' He formed a smile for Christine, but she didn't feel it was genuine.

'No trouble today?' Sophie asked.

He looked momentarily confused, then realised what she meant. 'No, no, all has been quiet.' He seemed distracted and kept glancing through the doorway the two women were heading for, as though watching for someone. Sophie's chat didn't seem to be wanted, so they carried on down through the room.

The windows onto the Charleton House gardens overlooked a large fountain, the lions carved into the base engaged in a frolic that could seem a little inappropriate. Beyond it, the rolling hills of Derbyshire framed the estate.

Mother and daughter continued into the 'carriages', a long corridor of baroque rooms with a railway carriage layout. The doors separating each one were in line with each other at one side of the building, so it was possible to stand with them all open and see right through to the far end, five rooms away. The rooms were panelled in dark wood, with views out over the elegant gardens. No matter the weather, they were always cold, and visitors never lingered very long.

Two staff, chatting up ahead, jumped apart when they saw the women approach.

'Oh, it's you. Hello, Sophie.'

Sophie laughed. 'Don't worry, I won't tell you off for chatting, especially when it's…' Sophie glanced at her watch, 'ten minutes before closing. You've not been too busy, I hope, Margaret?' She directed the question at a sprightly looking grey-haired woman who was dressed differently to the other visitor assistants. The red fleece jacket and green rucksack she carried marked her out as a first aider, so she wasn't restricted to one room or section of the house and would respond to radio calls for assistance anywhere.

Margaret shook her head.

'A child with a grazed knee, another one who got a paper plane in their eye during an education session, and a member of staff who scalded themselves with the water for a Pot Noodle. A quiet day in all.'

'That'll teach them for not coming and getting their lunch from you,' Christine said to Sophie, and then to no one in particular, 'A Pot Noodle of all things. I didn't think people still ate those.'

'Well, I think after today, they have one less fan,' said Margaret. 'He didn't look keen to try again.'

'Remind him where the cafés are, I promise it's safer,' said Sophie.

'And healthier,' added the woman who had been chatting with Margaret. Sophie smiled at her.

'Sally, you remember my mum, don't you?'

'Of course,' the woman said, turning to Christine, 'you came to the bank holiday fair, didn't you? I seem to recall we chatted about begonias at the plant stall.'

After the two women had exchanged a few more words about their favourite plants, Sophie led her mum on to the next room in the carriages. It was a bedroom draped in luxurious pinks, reds, and golds. From the ornate fabrics on the four-poster bed, to the fine red damask of the curtains, to the deep pink velvet on the walls, this room was less about comfort and more about a display of wealth. The bed had been at Charleton House for 300 years, from when it was commissioned especially for the Duchess of Ravensbury of the time.

'I bet this bed was made every morning.' Christine looked at Sophie out of the corner of her eye.

'Dear God, are you ever going to let that go?' They both laughed. 'I was never a morning person. Even now I can't function unless I've had a gallon of coffee.'

'Too much coffee, by my reckoning. You should cut back. Try some herbal tea, or decaffeinated coffee if you must.'

'Blasphemy, Mother, blasphemy.' Sophie formed a cross with her fingers and started to back away.

'Has this moved?' Christine looked at the bed. 'Only I don't remember it from my last visit and it's not exactly easy to miss.'

'It's just been put back after some conservation work. Isn't it gorgeous? Mind you, it's not the most interesting thing about this room.'

'Don't tell me there's a hidden watch in one of these paintings?'

'No, even better than that. It's got its own security system. Come over here.' Sophie led her mother to the side of the bed and pointed at two slim ropes that were hanging side by side, within reach of the occupant. 'There wouldn't have been a lot of privacy in here for the Duchess, with servants coming and going, and the Duke demanding her time, which she wasn't keen on giving as he was very unattractive inside and out. She wanted greater control over her privacy, and being a duchess, she didn't want to have to get out of bed to lock the doors, so she had these ropes installed. Each one is connected to a latch on the doors, and she would pull the rope to secure or release them. That way, even if someone had a key to the room, they couldn't get in. She was renowned for having affairs, so they probably got a lot of use.'

'Do they still work?'

'Perfectly.'

Christine followed the path of each rope, with her eyes finally resting on the very simple door latches that would drop into place.

'Ingenious. I could have done with one of these when you were a child and wouldn't go to sleep in your own bed.'

'We should get a move on,' said Sophie, apparently deciding to ignore her mother's teasing. 'They're going to start closing the house soon.'

They continued walking through the carriages into a dark wood-lined room with a small wooden bath tub.

'I'm impressed there was running water back in...' Christine peered at the information board '...1714.'

'Only cold water, though. The hot water still had to be brought up the backstairs. The tub was lined with linen sheets and fitted with a stool for the Duchess to sit upon as she soaped herself, and then had water scooped up and tipped over her.'

'I think they've overdone the special effects,' said Christine as she sniffed and wrinkled her nose.

'What do you mean, special effects?'

'Smellovision or whatever you call it – the smell that's pumped into a room to make it more authentic to what it would have been like all those years ago.'

'I wasn't aware that they did, and I can't smell anything special.' Sophie's expression turned from confusion to surprise. 'Mum, what is the scent you can smell?'

'Lavender. Very strong lavender.'

'You're kidding, right?'

'Why would I? I know what lavender smells like. Can't you smell it?'

'No, Mum, I can't.'

Christine knew she wasn't joking. 'Then what...'

'Apparently, some people can smell lavender in here. It was a favourite scent of the Duchess and it's believed to be her, just reminding people of her presence.'

'Smelloghost, then?'

'Sort of, yes, I guess you could call it that.'

Christine felt decidedly unnerved. She didn't typically believe in the supernatural, but there was no mistaking the smell, or the serious look on her daughter's face. She was in no rush to meet a duchess, past or present.

'Right, well, isn't it time we went?'

CHAPTER 2

The two women eventually made their way out onto a dark staircase with equally dark wooden panelling, and a strong musty smell that no one could miss. In the distance they heard the crackle of radios and the faraway sound of a heavy wooden door being closed. Sophie checked her watch.

'They're closing up. We can go back to my office to collect my things, and then we'll leave through the back. Dinner at mine?'

'Sounds wonderful.' Christine linked her arm through Sophie's and they descended the stairs, but before they ventured into the fresh air of the courtyard, a visitor assistant appeared through the doors.

'Oh, hello, Sophie. Don't fancy being locked in and spending the night with a few of our paranormal residents, then?'

'Not a chance. Clive, meet my mum. Clive is one of the longest-serving visitor assistants, and very partial to toasted teacake every morning.'

Clive smiled. 'They are rather a weakness, and if Sophie ever runs out, I don't know what I'll do.'

They chatted for a few minutes about Clive's thirty years at

Charleton House, the changes he had seen and what he had planned for his upcoming retirement. They were laughing about his love of steam engines and self-described status as a train geek when his radio burst into life and a familiar voice could be heard shouting.

'I need help, now, in the red bedroom. Help, she's not moving, I can't see her breathing. I need a first aider. Margaret?'

They all looked at one another, and then Clive set off, running up the stairs in the direction Rick's voice had come from, retracing the route that Sophie and her mother had just taken. The two women followed. Christine set an impressive pace and she reached the door before Clive.

They had been able to run through the last couple of rooms of the carriages as the doors were still open, but the large wooden door into the red bedroom was locked. Clive rattled the handle, but the door wouldn't budge.

'Do you have a key?' asked Christine.

'No, but Paul, the front of house manager, will have. He should have reached the other door by now, so I don't know why no one's unlocking this one.'

'Let me see.' Christine bent down and peered through the keyhole. 'She's on the floor, not moving.'

'Who is it?' asked Clive.

'No idea. I can't see her head, but it looks like she's in a uniform, so she's one of your lot.'

Shouts could be heard from the far door and Christine saw it move a little as a thud hit it. A different voice, sounding much calmer and more composed than Rick's, came across the radio. It sounded as though a manager had finally reached the other side, presumably Paul. As Christine stepped back from the door, he was asking for the help of security, someone from maintenance and checking that a first aider was on their way.

'Nearly there,' came Margaret's voice, slightly out of breath, over the radio.

Clive pulled a small penknife out of a pocket; he didn't appear to be keen to wait for anyone.

'Never know when this might come in handy.'

'You can't damage the door, there'll be hell to pay,' warned Sophie.

'I won't damage anything. I've done this before, but don't tell anyone.' He slid a blade down the gap between the door and the frame. 'A kid got himself stuck in there once because he was playing with the latch, and he started to panic. We couldn't calm him down and get him to follow our instructions, and waiting for help was going to take too long.' Clive gently moved the knife up and down as he spoke. 'None of these doors are perfect now, they're so old, and with this one there's a bit of a gap. If I just...' His tongue stuck out the side of his mouth as he focused intently on a tiny movement. With an almost imperceptible little flick of his knife, there was a clunk as the metal latch flipped up and released.

All three of them burst into the room. Christine and Sophie went straight to the woman lying on the floor, and Clive to the far door where he released the catch, allowing Rick and a man in a suit to enter. Christine immediately recognised the woman as Sally, the visitor assistant they had chatted to earlier. And she was convinced that Sally was dead.

Certain that there was no chance of reviving Sally, Christine nonetheless busied herself checking for a pulse, calling her name, trying to get some kind of response. She was relieved when she heard Margaret's voice and then felt the touch of a hand on her shoulder.

'I'll take a look. Sally, can you hear me, love?' Margaret rested two fingers on the woman's neck, then put her ear near her mouth. 'Sally, love, it's Margaret.' It was only as Christine stepped back to let Margaret do her work that she noticed the pool of blood under Sally's head and saw that it was slowly growing.

Christine went and sat on the stone windowsill out of the

way. The manager who had come through the other door with Rick was standing at a distance on his phone, answering questions and giving instructions, occasionally asking Margaret to verify some information as she performed CPR on Sally. Clive and Rick stood in the far corner, frozen, Clive with his hand on Rick's arm, offering some kind of shocked comfort. Together, they all formed a tableau like the ones Christine had seen in paintings around the house.

Margaret, clearly experienced, was calm, despite attending to the body of a seemingly dead colleague. And there was Sophie, kneeling by her side, ready to assist. Christine knew all about the dead bodies Sophie had encountered in her time working at Charleton House, but it had always been like listening to a rather fanciful tale when her daughter told her about her latest exploits. Not that she hadn't believed Sophie, just that it had all seemed unreal.

Christine was still sitting on the windowsill when the paramedics arrived and took over. Sophie came and sat beside her. Margaret – after speaking to one of the paramedics – sat on the other side. Clive and Rick made their way over, as though there was safety in numbers.

'She didn't stand a chance,' said Margaret matter-of-factly. As unflustered as she sounded, Christine could tell from a quick glance that she had been affected by trying to save her colleague. She looked tired and pale, not the rather strident woman Christine had been introduced to earlier. Years of being a first aider were unlikely to prepare you for seeing the body of someone you knew well. Margaret probably dealt with more corns and cuts than corpses.

Margaret reached for a screwed-up sweet wrapper that had been discarded on the windowsill.

'Disgraceful. Some people just don't care, do they.'

'That wouldn't have been Sally,' said Clive. 'She hated it when people left rubbish in the rooms, it made her really cross, and she always picked it up.'

Margaret put the wrapper in her pocket, and then sat quietly watching the paramedics. It was Clive who broke the silence when he let out a long, loud groan.

'I don't believe it, they can't have done. Well, at least we know why this happened.'

Christine followed the direction that Clive was looking in. There was a small space on the wall, a slight change in the shade of the fabric covering showing quite clearly that there had once been a painting there. Whichever painting it was that had been stolen, though, Christine was sure it wasn't valuable enough to have cost a human her life.

'We should leave them to it.' Paul had put his phone away and walked over to them. 'The police are probably going to want us out of here anyway.'

As if on cue, a familiar face came into the room. After scanning the occupants, his eyes rested on Sophie and gave a very slight roll.

'Not you again.' He paused and looked at Christine. 'I expected to see Sophie, but I didn't think this would be your idea of a fun day out.'

'Hello, Joe. It appears to be like mother, like daughter,' said Christine, giving a wry smile. 'Now where would you like us? I'm sure you have some questions.'

'In the Library Café,' said Detective Sergeant Joe Greene, glancing at Sophie. 'I know someone who makes a good cup of coffee.'

CHAPTER 3

'You didn't see anyone leave when you ran up the stairs?' asked Joe as he took the cup of coffee from Sophie's outstretched hand.

'No, no one.'

Christine shook her head to confirm Sophie's response, and then spoke. 'And Sally was by the door, so no one could have slipped out without getting really close to us. We would have seen them.'

'Does this mean it's definitely murder?' asked Sophie. Joe shrugged.

'Not sure. She's clearly been hit on the head, but right now I don't know whether that's the result of a fall. I'm hoping the paramedics can give me a better idea.' He looked at his phone as though willing it to ring.

'Sally's always seemed so nice, though. She chats to me whenever I'm walking through the house, and my café staff love her. Why would someone want to kill her? Do you think her death is linked to the painting that appears to have been stolen? Do you think she disturbed the thief? The paintings aren't that important, surely?'

'Fear that they'd be identified?' suggested Christine. 'A horrific case of wrong place at the wrong time?'

'That's most likely,' said Joe, 'unless we discover some connection between Sally and the thefts, but I'd be surprised if that happens.'

After Joe had left to return to the crime scene, Christine was suddenly hit with a wave of exhaustion. She felt too tired to move, and wondered why she hadn't accepted the invitation of her neighbour to go to the garden centre that afternoon. That way, neither she nor Sophie would have been near the body, as this was meant to be Sophie's day off.

She forced herself to sit up straight as Paul walked into the café.

'Any chance of a coffee, Sophie?' he asked. 'I don't think I'm going to be going home any time soon.'

'Of course, come and join us. This is my mum, Christine. Mum, this is Paul, the front of house manager. He's in charge of the visitor assistants. Obviously, I didn't get a chance to introduce you earlier.'

They shook hands.

'How are you, Mrs Lockwood?' asked Paul.

'Christine, please. A little shocked, but I'm alright. This must be very difficult for you and your team, had Sally worked here long?'

'Twelve years, give or take. Yes, they took it hard when I told them. I gathered them all together, as they were still scattered about the house going through the closing procedures, wondering what was going on. They'd picked up some information over the radio, but after the initial alert, I switched to a different channel and used my phone so they weren't aware of everything. The news will spread now, and I'll speak to tomorrow's team first thing.'

'Was it an accident?' asked Christine.

'I hope so. There wasn't anything in the room that appeared to be a weapon – not that I could see, anyway.'

'And, of course, there's something more significant than that,' said Christine as Sophie returned with a coffee for Paul and a plate of ginger biscuits. 'There wasn't anyone else in the room, and both doors were locked using those old latches, so how could she have been killed?'

'I can't imagine her giving herself that blow to the back of the head,' said Paul.

'So, you think she fell, Mum?' Sophie didn't sound entirely convinced.

'Not everyone who dies within half a mile of you is murdered, Sophie. There might still be a few accidental deaths occurring in Derbyshire.' Christine's tone was gently mocking.

Sophie ignored the comment. 'But why would Sally lock the doors from inside?' she asked. 'Is that part of the routine, Paul?'

'No, not at all. At that point of the day, none of the doors should be closed, let alone locked. Rick hadn't reached her.'

'What do you mean, Rick hadn't reached her? What kind of routine?' asked Christine.

'It's the way we close the house. One staff member does various tasks in the room or rooms that they are responsible for that day, then locks up and moves along to the next room to meet the next staff member, and they move on together. This is repeated from room to room so that the person who initiates the process can check everything is secure and no visitors or staff get locked in overnight. They have a set of keys and they lock each room as they go along, gathering staff up.

'At the end of each series of rooms, with the staff all gathered, the initiator radios the security office to let them know that their route, as we call it, is clear and locked. Each group of staff then makes their way to a central point where I thank them for their work during the day, give them any information they might need and send them on their way.

'Sally should have been joined by Rick, and then they would have made their way down the stairs to meet Clive, but Rick said when he had finished checking the rooms he was responsible for, he found the door to the red bedroom closed and locked. He eventually looked though the keyhole and saw Sally on the floor, which was when he radioed in a panic.'

'Oh heck, of course! Rick found her first. That must have been particularly awful for him,' said Sophie.

'Why particularly awful?' asked Christine.

'Because Rick and Sally used to be married,' explained Paul. 'It was tough for a while. When they were going through the divorce, they didn't want to be near one another, and we had to manage the schedule so they weren't working together. We couldn't keep doing that, but luckily, they started to find it easier to be around one another and developed an amicable working relationship.'

'Are you sure?'

'What do you mean, Sophie? They were getting on fine as far as I know. Better friends than spouses, it seems.'

'Well, he was the one who found her, kind of, and it's often said that the person who finds the body is likely to be the killer. And most people are murdered by someone they know.'

Christine looked doubtful. 'Even if you exclude the fact that there was no apparent way he could have been in the room with Sally in order to kill her, we don't know for sure that she's been murdered.'

'Yes, we do.' They all turned round to look at Joe who had walked in on the end of the conversation. 'She didn't fall, she was hit on the back of the head. It was definitely murder.'

CHAPTER 4

'An impossible murder,' said Christine, alone with her daughter for the first time since all the drama of the day had started.

'But at least we have one suspect already.'

'Oh, Sophie, don't tell me you're going to get involved in this one too. Let Joe do his job. You must drive him up the wall.'

'Maybe, but I also drive the police's conviction rate up.' Christine knew Sophie was joking. She had never actually thought of her reputation as a super sleuth in that way; she wasn't inclined to take much in the way of glory, plus she tended to play down her involvement for fear of a slapped wrist from Joe's boss. 'Anyway, I don't choose to get involved in these things, they sort of happen around me. And don't tell me you're not curious.'

'About how someone could get in and out and leave the doors locked on the inside? Yes, but who did it, well, that's for the police to decide.' There was a pause while the two women were lost in their thoughts, then, 'I wonder if Rick could have killed her. Perhaps he harboured some lingering resentment from the divorce.'

'See!' exclaimed Sophie. 'You can't help yourself, you want to know who did it too.'

'I am mildly curious, but mildly is all.'

'So, you think Rick could have done it?'

'He has a possible motive, and when we spoke to him earlier, he didn't look very happy. He kept glancing through the door in the direction of Sally, like he was annoyed about something.' Christine thought for a moment. 'But surely, it's related to the theft. A painting was taken from the room at the same time a murder was committed, and that can't be a coincidence.'

Sophie nodded. 'But the painting could have been taken before the murder occurred... ah no, that couldn't be. The staff are all on pins, terrified of another theft happening.'

Christine tapped the side of her face, a sure sign that she was thinking very deeply about something. 'What if it *was* taken when the room was locked, but only to throw the police off track?' she mused. 'Of course, they are going to think that the thief was caught in the act, killed Sally, and then took the painting. That way, the police keep looking at the clues they already have regarding the thefts, which would lead them away from the murderer. That would mean it was someone who knew about the thefts at the very least.'

'The thefts aren't a secret so that could be anyone,' said Sophie. 'I know that Joe finds the whole thing rather embarrassing, with his girlfriend working here.'

Christine had to accept she was enjoying this, knocking ideas about with her daughter. Admittedly, it would have been more appropriate to spend their time together discussing the colour for a new set of curtains, or whether the last series of *Vera* had been any good, but who cared what was appropriate when a murder needed solving?

'Do we know anything else about Sally?' she asked. 'Was there anyone here at Charleton House who didn't like her?'

Sophie smiled. 'I don't know, but we can find out.'

Paul was alone in his office when Sophie and Christine found him. His tie was loose and hanging at an odd angle, his sleeves had been hurriedly rolled up and he looked exhausted. Paul's office was quite large and looked out over a pretty courtyard, but it desperately needed a coat of paint, and one of the shelves on the bookcase was collapsing and being held up by a cardboard box.

'I know it's awful, but I've had to direct all my phone calls through to voicemail,' he told them. 'I'm getting so many calls from staff who have heard the news, and I just can't take it anymore.'

'It was the right thing to do,' said Christine, resting her hand briefly on his shoulder as she sat on a chair at the side of his desk. 'You're going to be no good to anyone else if you don't take care of yourself first. You can talk to people in the morning. Gossip travels fast anyway, so it won't be long before everyone will know.'

'Oh yes, and particularly with this team. They're hard workers, but they have a lot of time to spend inside their own heads while they're stood out in the rooms, especially when it's quiet. Gossip is one of the things that ends up filling their time.'

'Is it harmless gossip or does it ever get more serious?' Christine sounded sympathetic, but she had an agenda.

'Usually harmless, but like any workplace, things can sometimes get a little out of hand. Someone's feelings get hurt, people fall out. Eventually, things come out in the wash and everything is fine, until the next time.'

'Was Sally the kind to gossip?' asked Sophie.

'Oh yes, absolutely. She'd got a few people's backs up over the years, but she also had a group of firm friends. Plus she'd been on the receiving end of a lot of talk when her marriage to Rick started to break down.'

'People took sides?'

'Definitely. I had to have a word with a few people cos it got a bit spiteful. In the end, Sally and Rick were the ones to calm it all down, which was surprising as it had been a very bitter split, but they went to marriage guidance to help them through the divorce, and over time, they were able to be in the same room together without fighting. Eventually, others took their lead, and everything settled down.'

'So, you don't think Rick had any lingering animosity towards Sally?'

'No, he… wait…' Paul looked at Christine with an expression of horror. 'You don't think he did this, do you? He wouldn't, he couldn't, how could he? It's impossible.'

'Someone did. We might not know how it was possible, but it happened, so someone figured out how to do it. Could it have been Rick?'

Despite his apparent shock at the idea of Rick killing Sally, Paul did seem to be giving the question some thought. Finally, he shook his head.

'I really don't believe he did. He has his faults, but he's not a killer.'

Christine glanced up at Sophie who gave a very slight shake of her head. It was time to leave Paul in peace, he'd had a difficult day.

As soon as they were outside, Christine looped her arm through Sophie's, a move that was instinctive to them both.

'So, what do you think, Mum?' Sophie asked. 'Do you think Rick did it out of some lingering animosity that he'd been storing up?'

'That's exactly what I think.'

'Surely it's a bit late to get rid of her now, they were divorced.'

'It doesn't mean that he didn't still hold a grudge against her, that getting on with her had been an act because he knew what was good for him, or because he thought it would deflect attention away from himself when he was finally able to get her alone and kill her. But we can't close our minds to other possibilities. We need to find out more and be absolutely certain.'

Sophie turned to face her mother. 'What happened to leaving

this to the police? What about all the advice you've given me over the last few years to stop playing detective and focus on cakes in case I get in too deep and find myself on the end of a killer's wrath? What happened to...'

'Alright, I'll admit it, this is rather addictive. Probably not very healthy, but it is fun.' Christine looked horrified and quickly placed her hand over her mouth. 'I shouldn't have said fun, that was awful. I take it back.'

Sophie laughed. 'I know what you mean, Mum.'

'Don't ever tell anyone I said that.'

'I promise.'

'You'd better not be crossing your fingers.'

Sophie waved her hands, with all fingers uncrossed, in the air. 'I promise. Now, come on. Let's see if we can catch Margaret, if she's not already left.'

CHAPTER 5

'I've never been inside the first-aid room in all the time I've worked here, which I suppose I should be grateful for. I mean, I've had days where I needed to lie down, but horizontally on a sun lounger with a cocktail because work was driving me nuts.'

Sophie knocked softly, but there wasn't a response. The door to the first-aid room was ajar, so Christine pushed it open and stepped inside. There was a metal-framed bed in the corner, some rather old and tired-looking armchairs, a line of filing cabinets and a number of cupboards which, she assumed, contained an array of medical equipment.

As they entered, Margaret was hanging up her red fleece in a cupboard. She spun around.

'Oh my, it's you! You made me jump.'

'Sorry, we should have made sure you knew we were here.' Christine felt terribly guilty. This was not the day to be surprising people.

'I thought I was going to be next,' said Margaret as she took a dramatic deep breath, then she pulled her shoulders back and regarded the two women with a serious expression. 'Right then, how can I help? Are you not feeling well?' She looked from

Sophie to Christine, apparently trying to determine which one of them needed her assistance.

'We're fine, we just wanted to talk to you.'

'Of course, if you don't mind me doing a few jobs while we talk. I'm afraid I'm rather behind after, well, everything that's happened.' Margaret had regained some of the colour in her face.

'Did you know Sally well?' Christine asked.

'We'd worked together for ten years so I knew her fairly well as a colleague. I wouldn't have called her a friend, though. Why do you ask?'

Mother and daughter glanced at one another. Sophie was the one to reply.

'We've just been thinking about who would have wanted to do this to her. It's just so awful, we can't get it out of our heads.'

'I know what you mean. I doubt I'll think about anything else tonight, or for a long while after.' Margaret had emptied out some of the contents of her green rucksack onto the table and was going through the first-aid kit she carried, ticking items off a list on a clipboard and occasionally crossing to a cupboard to get something to add to the pile. 'The visitors all loved Sally. She knew the history of this place inside out and could really capture people's attention. She was particularly good with the children.'

'How did she get on with the other staff?' Christine made herself comfortable in one of the armchairs. The leather let out a rather unfortunate noise as she sat down and she saw Sophie try to hide a snigger. *Child,* she mouthed at her.

'Well enough, most of the time.'

'What do you mean?' asked Sophie.

Margaret sighed. 'I really don't like speaking ill of the dead, but Sally could be, well, challenging.' She paused. 'She was passionate about this place, there's no doubt about that, and she did a great job, but she liked to get recognition for that.

'Don't get me wrong, we all like to be told we're doing well, but her determination to be praised for every tiny thing she did just became irritating. She'd make complaints if she didn't feel that she was being treated like the star of the day, which got very tiresome for everyone else.'

Christine nodded, but to her, this didn't seem like a motive for murder.

'She was forever sticking her nose into other people's business. She liked to be seen as some kind of mother figure, so she'd befriend the newest and quietest members of staff and pull them into her little coterie of Sally fans. When she warned them to stay away from someone just because she had an issue with that person, it was quite destructive. She would also take on crusades, like wanting a new way of allocating annual leave because she felt the current one wasn't fair, even though none of the rest of us agreed.'

Margaret looked across at the two women and smiled. 'Ridiculous, I know, but she could just be really annoying, and when her latest crusade had gone on for a while, some of the team would get very irritated with her. I can't think of anyone who would want to kill her, though, despite many people probably having joked about it. But she might have pushed someone a bit too far.'

Margaret shook her head sadly. 'I suppose her heart was in the right place a lot of the time, and whatever anyone thought of her, she's leaving behind a big hole.'

Christine felt a bit deflated. It wasn't impossible that Sally had rubbed someone up the wrong way too many times and they had finally flipped, but that seemed to leave a lot of people with a motive, even if it was a weak one. She also wasn't sure if the use of the latches in the bedroom was a sign of planning or just quick thinking, a sudden attack when someone momentarily lost it, annoyed with their colleague.

Margaret looked tired and Christine felt bad for preventing her from getting home. After some polite words reminding her to take care of herself, with Sophie recommending a hot toddy and an early night, they got up to leave.

'Are you going to be OK?' asked Sophie. 'Will you be on your own tonight?'

Margaret shook her head. 'I live with my brother, so I'll be fine.'

'Good. He'll look after you, I'm sure.'

She raised an eyebrow. 'Doubt it. But no, I won't be alone.'

CHAPTER 6

Mother and daughter walked wearily to the car park, each lost in their own thoughts. Sophie's phone beeped and she stopped to read the text message.

'Mark and Joyce are in the pub,' she said. 'Fancy having dinner there?'

Christine's eyes lit up. She needed a good meal, but had been feeling bad about Sophie having to cook.

'I think that sounds wonderful, and I haven't seen Joyce in ages. I always love to see what she's wearing.'

'That's a very polite way of saying it, Mother.'

'Alright,' Christine grinned cheekily, 'I can't wait to see what clown costume she's got on today.'

The Black Swan pub was quiet and Christine soon spotted some familiar faces at what she knew was Sophie's favourite table: close to the log fire, but not too close; a good view of the door so they could watch who came in, but not close enough to feel a draught every time it opened; in a corner dark enough to be cosy, but near enough to a window not to feel gloomy. Joyce had her usual glass of champagne in front of her, Mark a dark beer.

'Ladies, please...' Mark leapt up and dramatically pulled out two chairs for them.

'Thank you, Mark, glad to see that chivalry isn't dead yet,' said Christine.

'You never did that for me,' complained Joyce with an equally dramatic flourish. 'Christine, lovely to see you again. Sophie, I'm hoping you'll pay for your mother's dinner.'

'Great.' Sophie rolled her eyes. 'I've been sat down for two seconds and you're ganging up on me. I don't know what I've done to deserve this.'

'You love it, Sophie. Now, what are you both drinking? Mark will fetch them for you.'

Mark leapt out of his seat once more and mimed pulling out a notepad and writing down their orders.

Eventually, with drinks fetched and the four of them able to relax, Christine took some time to give Joyce the once-over while the other three discussed the day's events. Her first thought was that Joyce had intentionally dressed like a tulip. A red silk shirt flowed loosely around her curves, but the large collar stood to attention, reaching to just below her ears like the plastic collar the vet would put around a dog's neck after an operation to ensure they didn't lick their stitches. The large yellow ceramic earrings Joyce wore looked like dabs of pollen. Christine couldn't see what Joyce was wearing below the waist and didn't think she wanted to know. If the skirt or trousers turned out to be green, then she wasn't sure she'd be able to contain herself.

'I think you're missing out a key suspect,' said Mark as he wiped beer foam off his perfectly coiffed moustache. They all waited in silence until Sophie gave up.

'Go on, then. Less of the suspense, we're talking about a killer here.'

'Well, I'd be very careful because you're sat next to her.'

Sophie glanced at her mother, and then at Joyce.

'It could go either way. Do you want to narrow it down for me?'

He nodded in Joyce's direction. Joyce didn't flinch, just continued to raise her champagne glass to her lips.

'Madam here didn't have a very good relationship with the victim.'

'That's not quite accurate. I simply refused to give her a job in retail.' Joyce managed the shops at Charleton House with a formidable reputation for being strict and blunt, but always fair minded.

'Why not?'

'She was boring, I don't like boring people. And I already knew she was a born whinger who would only stir up trouble.'

'Well, she still managed to do that for you,' said Mark.

'No, she didn't. She made a few ridiculous comments about me not giving her a fair chance, said she was going to make a complaint against me, but I ignored her childish outbursts and eventually she moved on to her next target. Anyway, you can be absolutely certain that I didn't kill her.'

Again, the group waited in silence, this time for Joyce to finish.

'She wasn't hung, drawn and quartered, and as you are all aware, if I am going to do something, I am going to do it properly and with a flourish.'

None of them could disagree with that, so no one replied. They all sat with their thoughts for a little while. It was Christine who was the first to speak and she directed her question at Joyce.

'You said Sally moved on to her next target, so who was that?'

'There are too many to count, but I'm pretty certain it was Paul.'

'Paul as in her manager?'

'Yes. I can't remember what the complaints were about, but that poor man would have the support of everyone who knew her if he had finally had enough and decided to put an end to things. It must have been absolute hell to manage her.'

Christine decided that a return visit to the house was in order the next day, and judging by the look she got from her daughter, Sophie was in agreement.

'Now, Christine,' Joyce shuffled herself into a more formal upright position, placed her glass on the table and gave Christine an intense look, 'there is something far more important than mere murder that we need to discuss.'

Christine mirrored Joyce's movements and prepared herself for whatever was about to come her way.

'We need to know your opinion on Sophie's new chap, Ryan. I presume you've met him?'

Sophie groaned and slouched into her chair, looking very embarrassed. Christine, on the other hand, didn't flinch.

'Well, Joyce, first of all, I have to say that I'm happy someone is on the scene. It is about time Sophie embarked on a relationship. I was beginning to wonder if Pumpkin would be the only living creature that she'd ever share a bed with...'

Mark snorted and narrowly missed spraying the table with beer.

'MUM! I am right here, you know.'

Christine gave her daughter a playful smile.

'And the choice of Ryan?' Joyce wasn't done yet.

'He seems like a very nice young man. Polite, smartly dressed, a bit skinny for my liking.'

'Hey, what's wrong with skinny?' Mark was the only person any of them knew who could give Ryan a run for his money in the scrawny stakes.

'Nothing at all, if you don't mind waking up next to a bag of bones,' answered Joyce.

Christine rested her hand on Sophie's. 'He's very nice.'

'Well, he's passed the "meet the mother" stage,' said Mark to Joyce, 'so I guess it's serious. When are we all going to spend some time with him, Sophie? You do realise that it can't actually be declared a *relationship* until he's passed an evening in here with Joyce and me. After we've completed our assessment, *if* we approve, then and only then can you consider yourself to be spoken for.'

'Do you really think I'm going to subject him to that?' Sophie wore a look of mock horror. 'He'll run a mile.'

'If he's not prepared to walk over hot coals or spend an evening in Joyce's company, whichever is the more painful, then he's not worthy of you.' Mark's tone was deadly serious.

'You've not met Ryan yet?' Christine was surprised.

'Briefly,' replied Joyce, 'but we haven't had a chance to get the thumbscrews out yet.'

After they had all devoured dinner and dessert – sticky toffee pudding all round – they got up to leave. The first thing Christine did was glance at Joyce. She smiled as she saw a pair of tightly fitting green trousers and couldn't resist humming 'Tulips From Amsterdam' to herself.

CHAPTER 7

Sophie, Christine, and Paul were sitting around a small table in the corner of his office. He had offered them both coffee, but Christine had spotted the jar of instant on the shelf. She couldn't imagine a situation that would cause Sophie to lower her standards that far south, so she had declined too.

Paul looked tired and Christine doubted that he had got much sleep. She briefly wondered if it was guilt that had kept him awake.

'How's the team?' Sophie asked. She had explained to her mum that Paul would have held their morning briefing by now, and if any of them lived on Mars, it would have been their first time hearing about the events of the previous evening.

'Still shocked, and very upset. Sally wasn't the most popular member of the team, but she was still one of them. We're very much like a family – a dysfunctional one, but a family all the same.'

Christine took in his neatly trimmed beard, crisply ironed shirt and the perfectly symmetrical knot in his tie, very different to how he had appeared at the end of the previous day. Paul was clearly a man who cared about appearances. She was wondering how they were going to broach the subject of Sally's complaints against him when Sophie spoke.

'It must be so hard, Paul, I can't imagine the range of emotions you'll be experiencing. I do hope you're looking after yourself.'

He smiled. 'Oh, I'll be fine. There is a lot to do at a time like this. We're making sure everyone has access to a counsellor if they need it, and the police will probably want to ask more questions. I'm sure I'll see the Duke and Duchess today.'

Sophie had told Christine just what good people the Duke and Duchess of Ravensbury were, so she had no doubt that they would prove themselves to be extremely considerate employers.

'I have heard you had your own challenges with Sally,' she said. 'There must be some sense of relief that the complaints will be dropped.' She clamped her mouth shut, realising what she had just said without any kind of gentle build-up.

'Oh, they were nothing, just Sally and… wait, how do you know?'

Christine was relieved when Sophie spoke.

'You know what gossip is like, Paul. That sort of thing comes bobbing to the surface at times like this, and I believe you're not alone in being targeted by Sally in that way. It must have been so stressful, though.'

Christine couldn't help but notice he had started to play with a ring on his finger, spinning it slowly around and around.

'It comes with the territory. When you're a manager, there will always be people who don't like you.' His jaw was becoming set. The subject of the complaints had clearly touched a nerve and he was working hard not to show it.

He stared at Christine for a moment. 'Why are you here? I mean, you're Sophie's mother, I know, but why are you…?' There appeared to be genuine confusion in his voice, but he seemed annoyed too.

'I am in education, helping young people problem-solve and deal with the stresses around that. It was felt that it might be useful if I stayed around during the first couple of days after Sally's death to assist should it be needed.'

Christine was trying not to catch her daughter's eye. She paused for a moment, hoping that Paul would keep talking if given the space. Her patience was rewarded.

'It was all ridiculous. Favouritism! A hostile work environment! I was doing my job, for heaven's sake. I have to manage people, tell them when they need to modify their behaviour. And as for favouritism, I bend over backwards to make sure that we don't hurt Sally's feelings. *Didn't* hurt her feelings. I was never going to treat her any differently, but she was so blasted sensitive that I'd often approach subjects carefully with her for fear she'd kick off and put in another complaint. It was exhausting.'

He paused and Christine wondered if he was going to stop, but there was clearly too much that he wanted to get off his chest.

'And as for fraternising with a female employee – that was how she put it, so pious – I went to the pub with someone who wanted some career advice. It was a busy pub that's popular with the team. If I was going to *fraternise*, don't you think I'd have chosen to take the girl somewhere we wouldn't be seen? It was ludicrous.

'Of course, once Sally made the complaint, which was spurious and wasn't something HR wanted to touch with a barge pole, it put ideas in people's heads. I know that there was a rumour going around that I wasn't to be trusted, and female members of staff should never be alone with me. Sally didn't start that, and it got out of hand in a way she couldn't control, but it all stemmed from her complaints and gossip. If she hadn't said anything, the rumour mill wouldn't have gone into overdrive.'

Paul had started to go red and was talking faster and faster. 'I can't believe all the things we did to placate that woman. She got very close to destroying my career.'

Then he came to a natural stop and disappeared into his

thoughts for a few moments before looking up at the two women.

'I didn't want her dead, if that's what you're thinking.'

'No, no, of course not,' Sophie said with a reassuring tone.

'A lot of people didn't like her,' said Paul, 'but she was one of us.'

CHAPTER 8

'You're a blooming maths teacher, Mum, and a *retired* maths teacher at that. Are you trying to get me fired?'

'I didn't lie,' said Christine calmly as she and Sophie walked away from Paul's office. 'I said I solve problems and help people solve them too, that's maths. You should have seen how stressed some children would get when they were struggling with something I'd set them. So, it wasn't a complete lie, just a bit of a fib.'

Sophie shook her head, a resigned look on her face. 'If the Duke and Duchess find out that my mother is questioning staff whilst pretending to be some sort of management consultant who was *not* brought in by the company, that HR knows nothing about your presence, and yet I'm not only fully aware of your little act, I'm with you while you do it, they'll fire me.'

'Don't be so overdramatic, Sophie, they won't fire you. Sally's murder is the focus of everyone's attention right now, especially how on earth her killer got into and out of that bedroom. How someone was able to commit murder and then disappear from a locked room will be the sole topic of conversation, they won't give me a second thought. Anyway, they are probably so used to you asking questions about murders, they think it's in your job description: *make coffee, bake cakes, find killers.*'

'Bake cakes? Make coffee? Is that what you think I do all day? Nothing about the responsibilities that come with managing multiple cafés, dealing with staff, budgets, let alone the pressure of working with the public and for a duke and duchess in one of the country's most magnificent historic houses.'

'Are you finished? You know very well I have the utmost respect for your career. How much coffee did you have this morning?'

'Not enough.'

'I was thinking the opposite.'

'No, definitely not enough.'

'Then let's get you topped up.' Christine took her daughter's hand and led Sophie towards one of her own cafés. 'Budgets, though? Please, dear, I know how bad at maths you are. You couldn't manage your own pocket money.'

Sophie let go of her hand and stormed off ahead. Christine couldn't help but laugh.

'So, what do you think?' Sophie asked her mum as they sat down in a corner of the café, away from any of the visitors, after Christine had apologised, with her fingers crossed, for her comments about Sophie's numerical skills. 'Is Paul our killer?'

'I believe there is a very strong chance he did it, more so than Rick. We just have to work out how.'

'It's a bit obvious, though, isn't it? He has a strong motive, he clearly has a temper, and with everything she had accused him of, it's too black and white.'

'Well, you're more experienced at this than me, but does everything have to be complicated, with a list of red herrings and forever being led down dead ends? The combination of location and opportunity is confusing enough, so maybe the identity of the killer is easy, and he is relying on the fact that no one would be able to work out how it was done to get away with it.'

Sophie thought for a moment. 'Paul started working here three years ago and our paths have crossed quite a bit. He's always seemed like a reasonable, experienced manager, but he was certainly very concerned with his reputation. Mind you, you'd expect that in the early stages of a job when someone is trying to establish themselves.'

'I'm not so sure. I know it's tempting to work out who did it, and then we might be able to work out how, but we could try it the other way round. How was a woman murdered when she was alone in a room bolted from the inside?' Christine's eyes widened as a thought struck her. 'Well, alone apart from…'

'Apart from what, Mum?' asked Sophie impatiently as Christine fell silent.

'Apart from the scent of lavender.'

Sophie stared at Christine in confusion for a while, then laughed incredulously. 'You think Sally was killed by the ghost of a 300-year-old duchess?' she said. 'Just when I thought you were getting good at this sleuthing game.'

Christine grinned. 'Well, you have to look at every angle, surely?' she said. 'But yes, I agree we need to stick with the physical evidence and leave the spirits beyond the veil.'

'That's more like it,' said Sophie. 'We should go back and look at the red room. The police are bound to be done with it by now.'

Christine gave a nod of agreement. 'Drink up, then,' she said. 'I've got lunch booked with a couple of *retired* teacher friends and it would be nice to solve this by then.'

CHAPTER 9

Christine and Sophie had returned to their seats on the windowsill of the red bedroom. It felt odd now that there wasn't any evidence of the previous day's incident. Only the fact that it was so quiet because these rooms had been closed to the public for the next few days gave any clue to the crime that had taken place in there.

'Paul, Rick, countless members of Sally's team. We're not getting very far narrowing down who the killer might be, are we?' Christine looked at her daughter. 'I understand why this could take a few days to work out. There's not much chance of solving it by lunchtime, is there? Not really.'

Sophie smiled.

'What?'

'Something tells me you're going to be a lot more interested and understanding if I end up involved in another murder investigation in the future.'

'If? Don't you mean when?'

'What are you doing here? These rooms are meant to be locked.' Joe appeared through one of the doors.

'Well, someone didn't do a very thorough job. They were all

*un*locked. Well, most of them.' Sophie put her hands in the air, making it clear it wasn't their fault. Christine didn't say anything about the set of keys that Mark had given them.

'Good job it's not a crime scene anymore. We finished with it this morning.'

'So, can I ask what the local constabulary are doing in order to find the killer as quickly as possible?'

'Are you mocking me, Sophie?'

'Never. But I am curious.'

'Only because you want to be sure you know everything we do, which is not going to happen.'

'Can't blame a woman for trying. I'm sure I'll find out one way or another.'

Joe looked too distracted to argue the point.

'We're poring over the CCTV footage from yesterday, trying to identify who came in with a bag that would have fitted that picture and its frame.' He continued to look around the room. 'How did they do it, where did they go? There's no room under the bed, the windows are all secured, there aren't any cupboards, there were people outside both doors, and no one could have got past them.' He looked up at the ceiling.

'What are you hoping to find up there?' asked Sophie. 'Someone still hanging from the chandelier, waiting for the opportunity to jump down and make a run for it?'

'Sophie, the poor man is doing his best.'

'Don't worry, Christine, I'm used to this kind of abuse. We've tried to recreate the series of events leading up to Sally's death,' Joe continued, 'but there weren't even any members of the public in the rooms along this side of the building who could have slipped out.'

'Are you sure?' asked Sophie, who received a stern look from her mother. 'No, I'm not being rude. Maybe someone hid elsewhere, right up to the last minute, and then managed to sneak in here and latch the doors.'

'It's not a bad idea, but it doesn't explain how they managed to get out.'

Christine continued to examine the room, looking closely at the window immediately behind her. There was nothing that could answer the burning question. But my, were the curtains beautiful.

'Should I be touching these?' she asked. Sophie glanced over.

'It's fine, they're not originals.'

It was Christine who broke the silence that settled on them.

'Joe, I think we need a first aider.'

'Are you OK, Mum?' asked Sophie as Joe walked over, looking concerned.

'Christine, are you not well?'

'I'm fine, but we'll all feel a lot better if we see Margaret.'

'What on earth are you talking about, Mum? You're worrying me.'

'Oh,' Christine shrugged, 'I know who killed Sally and I reckon we can get that painting back too.'

CHAPTER 10

Mark placed four glasses on the pub table and joined the three women. Christine noted that Joyce didn't resemble a tulip today; based on the amount of animal print in her outfit, she belonged in a zoo, not a garden.

'At least we know where Sophie gets her sleuthing skills from, Christine,' Mark said. 'And you solved it so quickly. We all thought it was impossible.'

'The problem was we all thought it was going to be a complicated explanation, but it was incredibly simple and relied entirely on everyone being distracted by Sally and her injuries. Not that her murder was planned. Sally was annoying, but she wasn't the target of an elaborate plot.'

'Tell them what gave it away, Mum.' Sophie was grinning, apparently proud of her mother's deductive skills.

'A chocolate wrapper.'

The confused looks on the faces in front of her told Christine she needed to explain. She took a large drink of white wine and made herself comfortable. She had to confess, she was rather enjoying this.

'When we entered the bedroom and were able to attend to

Sally, it was a bit chaotic, but despite that, the killer couldn't have escaped then. We were right by the door on our side, and Paul and Rick were coming through the other door, so we would have seen them.

'Now, Margaret joined us a couple of minutes later and started administering first aid. We didn't question her appearance because we knew she was on the way, she'd said so over the radio. The thing to remember is that you can say you're in one place on a radio, but actually be in another, and how would we know?'

'So, where was she, then?' asked Mark, who was sipping his drink without paying proper attention and getting froth on his moustache.

'She was already in the bedroom,' said Christine, as if it was the most obvious thing in the world. 'When Margaret and Sophie sat on the windowsill with me after the paramedics had taken over, Margaret picked up a piece of rubbish, a chocolate wrapper. She made rather a point of it; I think she was trying to distract us from the fact that the curtains were in disarray. You see, she had been hiding behind them.'

'Why?' demanded Joyce. 'What was the woman doing there?'

'Why? Because Sally caught her stealing the painting. Margaret had the ideal way of getting the paintings out of the rooms without anyone knowing: she was hiding them in her first-aid rucksack. She would put them in a cupboard in the first-aid room until everything had calmed down, and then she would take them home in her own time.

'But this time, she was caught, by Sally. Margaret swung at her with the painting in a panic and killed her. She didn't mean to, I'm sure. Then, while trying to work out what to do next, she remembered the latches. She latched both doors so no one could get in for a while, which gave her time to think. Then she hid behind the curtains.

'When she was called over the radio, she replied saying she

was on the way and pretended to be out of breath so we thought she was running to the red room. Once the room was filling with panicked people, she took the opportunity to slip out from behind the curtain and pretend that she had just arrived. None of us noticed, we were too focused on Sally.'

'So, Sally wasn't really the target,' continued Sophie. 'Her death was an unintended consequence of Margaret stealing another painting.'

'Why would she be foolish enough to steal from her own employer?' Joyce had clearly made her judgement on Margaret. 'Surely, she knew she was going to get caught in the end. It's just sheer stupidity.'

'Money, I would guess,' said Christine. 'She happened to mention that she was living with her brother, and she didn't sound happy about it, so I doubt it was something she'd have done willingly. I think she was having money problems and she thought this was the only way out. And I agree, it was very stupid.'

Christine drained her glass. 'Well then, I should leave you all to it.' She stood up and put on her jacket. 'I know you are expecting a special guest.'

Mark and Joyce looked at one another, clearly clueless about what was happening.

'Sophie, you haven't told them?'

'I didn't want to give them time to plan an interrogation, so I thought that springing it on them might be best.'

'Will one of you please tell us what you're talking about?' Joyce didn't have a lot of patience at the best of times.

'Ryan,' said Sophie. 'Ryan is joining us imminently, as this way you two can't plan any kind of tactical approach.'

'Oh, Sophie,' said Joyce, winking at Christine and pretending to search through her bag. 'You must have realised by now that I never go anywhere without a pair of thumbscrews.'

THE JOYCE AND GINGER MYSTERIES

KEEP READING TO ENJOY THE FIRST THREE CHAPTERS NOW...

CHAPTER 1

'What I still don't understand is why we're staying in a hotel so close to our homes. We could just go for dinner, prop up the bar for a few hours, then I could get a taxi back to the comfort of my own bed. This seems like a rather pointless exercise to me.'

Joyce looked over at Ginger with a weary expression. They'd often talked about having a girls' weekend away together, but Joyce had meant heading down to London, or perhaps jumping on the Eurostar and enjoying the charms of Parisian men as they dined on a bateau-mouche with the Eiffel Tower above them. Not driving half an hour down the road from where she worked and staying in a town she knew like the back of her hand. Like the back of both hands and both her feet, come to think of it.

'Because, my dear, you don't have to make the bed in the morning. Because you don't have to make your own coffee, you can have breakfast brought to your room. Because there will be an entire cocktail bar at our disposal, and because my good friend is the manager of the hotel and he's invited me to stay for free and I've had the good heart to invite you along as my plus one. Although I can drop you off at a bus stop and go on my own if you'd prefer.' Ginger started to indicate and slow the car down as they neared a concrete box of a bus station up ahead.

Joyce wasn't up for a bus ride. 'There is something seriously wrong with the world the day I get on a smelly, germ-ridden tin can. I'm assuming we get a room each? I imagine you're a snorer.'

Ginger crunched through the gears as she increased the speed again. 'Of course.' It didn't escape Joyce's notice that Ginger didn't seem entirely confident in her response, but Joyce wasn't planning on accepting anything less than her own room. She could always deal with that at reception.

Joyce hadn't known Ginger for very long. The two single women, both in their late sixties, had met the previous year and over numerous glasses of champagne had discovered that despite being wildly different in almost every way, they made good, if rather odd, friends. Ginger, a sturdy woman who repaired her own garden walls and refused to buy clothing that had special washing requirements (silk being an exception to the rule), and Joyce, who spent more time over her makeup each morning than Ginger spent in a typical year, had found in one another comfortable companions. Conversation had quickly turned to weekends away, but with spa breaks being Joyce's preferred choice, while a weekend tramping over the mountains of the Lake District or exploring the history of a city with a guide book in one hand formed the basis of Ginger's suggestions, time had flown and nothing had come of the plans. Until Joyce got a phone call.

'Pack up your lipsticks, unplug your hair straighteners, and get ready to relax. We have an all-expenses-paid weekend in a newly renovated hotel with an excellent cocktail bar.' Joyce hadn't questioned the free aspect of it; she was all in. She just hadn't expected her dreams of Monaco or Vegas to be interrupted with, 'We're off to Buxton.'

'Buxton?' she had screeched. Even Joyce had to admit that it was a screech. 'I do my shopping in Buxton. If I need to go inside an actual bank, I go to Buxton. I do not go to Buxton for a weekend of glamour and relaxation.'

'We've always talked about going away together. If it turns out that we drive each other up the wall, this is a whole lot easier than trying to avoid each other for a weekend when we're somewhere like Madrid, and then having to sit next to each other on the plane home, fighting wordlessly over the arm rest. Glamour is all in the mind, love, it's all in the mind.'

'It's all in your bloomin' mind if you think I'm coming,' Joyce had muttered.

'I heard that, you ungrateful madam. I'll pick you up from work next Friday at 4pm.'

'We don't close the shop until six.'

'You're the boss. Get someone else to do it.'

Joyce couldn't argue with that. She was in charge and never shied away from delegating if she needed to pop out to buy a new pair of shoes ("need" being a relative word; she owned over 200 pairs) or her favourite mascara was running low.

'Alright,' she'd grumbled. 'Only I'm not going up any bloody hills for one of your afternoon rambles.'

Joyce now looked across at Ginger. 'You better be right about the extensive cocktail bar. Alcohol might be the only interesting thing about this weekend.'

Ginger brushed her rather wild and undisciplined grey hair out of her eyes, and Joyce was left distinctly uncomfortable by the smirk she was convinced she had seen flit across her friend's face. She sank into the seat for the remaining fifteen minutes' drive and closed her eyes, clinging on to the vision of a yacht bobbing in the waters of St Tropez. Dreading whatever reality waited for her up the road, she was going to take every available minute to indulge in her dreams.

In truth, Joyce had always been fond of Buxton, one of England's finest Georgian spa towns. Perhaps not quite as well-known as Bath, it is still a tourist destination, flocked to by lovers of Austen and Brontë who like to imagine Mr Darcy popping by to enjoy the healing properties of the famous thermal waters. That was something that Joyce could relate to; she could easily view herself among the wealthy visitors of the 18th century. Of course, running into Mr Darcy also featured in her imaginings. He would invite her to a ball, and later accompany her to a salon or some theatrical entertainment at the Opera House, which would likely result in more racy memories than her recent visit with Ginger. After watching a rather fine Gilbert and Sullivan, Joyce had been subjected to Ginger's high-pitched declaration that she was a *Modern Major General* for the entire drive home and it had taken all her willpower not to steer them under an oncoming bus.

It had never crossed Joyce's mind to stay in Buxton itself, no matter how late some of the events she had attended finished. She would just call a taxi and enjoy the silk sheets of her own queen-sized orthopaedic alpaca-hair mattress, knowing that she could drink her favourite coffee and luxuriate in her favourite bath salts the following morning. Having said that, she did quite like the idea of a change of scenery. The gloom of January and February had started to seep into her bones. She'd managed a week on the island of Majorca at the start of the year, but the vitamin D boost she'd received had long since dwindled, and she'd resorted to pulling out the brightest of her clothes from her comprehensive wardrobe. Her yellow twinset with stylish black edging and buttons and a matching skirt had resulted in one particularly annoying colleague referring to her as a bumble bee, and her rainbow-striped woollen dress had the same cretin asking her if a pot of gold could be found under its pleats. The sniggers and range of innuendos had lasted the rest of the week. But if nature was not feeling duty bound to liven up the monochrome weather that had been blanketing the hills of Derbyshire, Joyce was more than equipped to do the job.

Now, however, she wanted a break. She hoped she possessed enough imagination to pretend that the hotel they were heading for was actually on New York's Fifth Avenue, if you ignored the northern English accents and the popularity of sausage rolls and fried breakfasts in the surrounding cafés.

Joyce's eyes popped open as she heard the squeal of tyres and the sound of Ginger shouting at another driver, informing him in rather crass tones what he could do with his Porsche SUV and where she was convinced it might fit. Joyce sank further down in her seat. It was bad enough that she had to be driven in a scratched, dented and muddy twenty-year-old three-door Ford Fiesta, her own convertible BMW currently undergoing repairs after Joyce had become a little too intimate with a wall so low it had almost been invisible, but now the language being tossed out of the window made the whole scenario more embarrassing than she thought possible. Once the driver of the SUV realised that Ginger was unlikely to be concerned about her car getting a few extra dents in a parking tussle, he drove off with a hand gesture which Joyce was sure couldn't be found in the dictionary of British Sign Language, and Ginger did a neat little reverse park into a space within sight of the front doors of The Lodge, their home for the weekend.

Joyce took a deep breath. *Imagine it's New York, imagine it's Paris*, she chanted to herself as her cherry-red lips formed a tight smile. She quickly checked her blonde hair to make sure the modern take on a beehive hadn't been damaged on the journey, convinced herself her makeup didn't need reapplying (unlikely – she'd done that thirty minutes ago), and then swung her rather impressively shapely legs out of the car. This might not be her dream destination, but she was going to make an entrance that told the staff what kind of weekend she was expecting.

CHAPTER 2

Ginger looked up at the entrance with pride. She felt a bond with The Lodge, having watched it grow from a large, well-respected, but slightly tired establishment into one of the most talked-about boutique hotels in the area. The Lodge was formed from a row of Victorian villas that looked out across the Pavilion Gardens, the final touches being added during a long-term renovation programme on the top floor which had left half the rooms closed over the winter. She had contributed to the work by making a number of curtains and cushions out of a fabric that the manager had found on his travels to India and Istanbul. Ginger's career as a seamstress had seen her making ornate costumes for West End musicals, so this had been a quick and easy job for a childhood friend.

With a large holdall slung over one shoulder and a bundle containing her coat, an extra cardigan which she'd thrown in the car at the last minute, two scarves and a pair of sheepskin gloves, Ginger leant her shoulder against the door and pushed her way through. The lobby immediately sucked visitors into its warm embrace, the mahogany reception desk taking centre stage against a backdrop of dark green walls. Contemporary artwork threw cooler colours and light into the room, each in elaborate gold frames. Two armchairs in gold fabric flanked a low table made from the stump of a tree, upturned so the roots carefully held a glass top, with flecks of gold scattered within the glass. The flamboyance of the space matched the personality of the family who owned the hotel.

Ginger heard 'Thanks' muttered from behind her, at which point she realised she had forgotten to hold the door open for Joyce, who was lugging an enormous lurid-pink suitcase behind her. Ginger might have guessed that she would have packed multiple outfit changes for each day.

'Oops, sorry, love. You alright?'

'Of course I'm alright. It...'

Ginger didn't catch the rest. She dropped the pile of clothes onto an armchair and threw her arms around the neck of a mountain of a man. Dennis Matty, the general manager and the latest of the generations of his family to run the hotel, was almost as broad as he was tall, and he was very tall. His impressive girth was clad in a beautifully tailored navy-blue pinstripe suit and deep pink tie, an outfit that Ginger could have described before she entered the building. It was his uniform of sorts; he had a wardrobe full of navy pinstripe suits and a vast collection of pink ties. Whether it was a shade of plain pink, had dots, stripes, or some other pink detail, each and every tie had a matching handkerchief which protruded from the breast pocket in a perfectly twisted triangle.

He gave Ginger a tight squeeze and lifted her briefly from the floor.

'Careful there, you'll do your back in.' Ginger laughed, although she wasn't kidding; she wasn't small herself. Whenever she was with Dennis, she felt like the teenager she, and he, had been when they first met.

'Never, you're as light as a feather.'

There was a soft snort and they turned together towards the door.

'I'm sorry, Dennis, this is Joyce Brocklehurst. Joyce, this is Dennis Matty.'

Dennis stepped past Ginger and took Joyce's hand in both of his, briefly examining the bright pink talons on the end of each finger. Ginger noted Joyce's appraisal of his appearance; she seemed satisfied. Dennis too seemed rather pleased with the vision before him. A dark-pink long-sleeved t-shirt with thick black and white swirls was topped off by a long pink coat. Black trousers which were a little too tight, pink shoes and a matching handbag finished off the look.

'Welcome, Joyce, I'm so pleased that Ginger brought you with her. It's going to be a pleasure to get to know you, and I want to hear all about life working for a Duke and Duchess.' His warm baritone voice echoed in the lobby. Everything about Dennis exuded warmth and familiarity.

'Oh, I only run their gift shops, it's nothing too fancy. It's lovely to meet you too, Dennis. When Ginger suggested a weekend in your fine establishment, it didn't take a moment's thought for me to accept. I've heard so much about your hotel and the word on the street is that you're doing a rather magnificent renovation.'

Ginger smiled to herself. Joyce had turned up the intensity on her 'Lady of the Manor' act. She was all Received Pronunciation and cut-glass vowels when she wanted to be, but she was a Derbyshire lass really, although the overworked enunciation didn't appear entirely out of place. With her sharp posture, chin up, designer handbag dangling from an arm held at a neat 90 degree angle and the whole display balanced on a pair of stilettos that could be used to spear fish, all Joyce lacked was a tiara, and Ginger guessed she probably had a couple of those at home.

'It's not so much a renovation as a redecoration, but I'm hoping the impact is as impressive. The upper floor was the only area yet to be refreshed and we're just having a few finishing touches done before it officially reopens on Friday. However...'

Ginger gave a small clap of her hands; she knew what was coming next.

'Yes, my dear, I've made sure two of the rooms have been finished for your arrival and you're in Mary's room. Joyce is next door.'

Ginger looked across at her friend. 'Mary, Queen of Scots. I've always wanted to stay in there, it's the most decadent room.'

'She didn't actually stay here,' Dennis explained to Joyce, 'she stayed over the road at the Old Hall, but I felt that an homage was in order, and it meant I could have a lot of fun with the whole Queen theme. Do you have all your bags? I'll carry them up for you, and then you can have some lunch.'

'No you won't,' Ginger instructed. 'We can carry our own bags. You can get busy at the bar; Joyce and I will be down for cocktails as soon as we've dropped our things off.' She saw a light come on in Joyce's eyes at the mention of cocktails.

'As you wish, madam, I will go and warm up.' He walked through a door, miming the actions of shaking a cocktail high in the air. Ginger laughed.

'Come on, Lady Muck, let's go and check out our home for the weekend. Sorry you didn't get the room fit for a queen. On this occasion, you get to be the lady's maid in the room next door.'

CHAPTER 3

Joyce breathed in the smell of fresh paint as they ascended the stairs. She wished that Dennis had opened a few more windows, but at least it was a sign that plenty of work had been going on. As the upper floor wasn't officially open to guests yet, she shouldn't be too surprised if she saw sheets still protecting carpets or plastic wrapping on furniture. They passed two young men who were on the way down the stairs, *Bennett's Family Carpenters* written on their t-shirts, and Joyce enjoyed the lingering look one of them gave her. She hadn't lost her touch.

The solid wooden banisters matched the mahogany desk, the staircase walls covered in a grey velveteen wallpaper with an ornate pattern that gave a shimmering effect. More pictures in gold frames lined the route. Once at the top floor, the wide staircase opened out onto an attractive bright landing, a large window overlooking the Pavilion Gardens opposite. The cast-iron and glass structures of the pavilion and conservatory were two of the many landmark buildings that pulled people to the pretty town. A velvet loveseat was positioned so visitors could sit and enjoy the view.

Ginger led the way, looking from behind like a washerwoman

heading to the laundry with the bundle of clothes in her arms. Joyce couldn't understand why she hadn't taken the time to fold them and add them to her bag. The picture wasn't helped by the loose skirt Ginger was wearing, which was now hanging at an odd angle, one side lower than the other, or the thick oversized fleece shirt she had put on to keep the cold out, making her look bigger than she really was.

Ginger's head turned at each room to check the name. On this floor, Joyce had noticed, the rooms were not numbered, but named: the Anne Lister; the Joseph Paxton; the Josiah Wedgwood. All names of famous people who'd held associations through the ages with Buxton or who had been known to visit, although some of the links were a little tenuous. It appeared that Dennis was a man who didn't mind playing fast and loose with history in the name of drama and fun.

A housekeeper's cart sat up ahead, just before a junction in the corridor, but there was no sign of the housekeeper.

'Here we are, Mary, Queen of Scots. This is mine; you're next door in Mr Wedgewood, so to speak.' Ginger handed Joyce a key with a soft leather tag, and then tried to insert another key into her own door. 'See you in a minute.'

'Hang on just one minute, lady. I want to check out your room first, so that when I do go into mine, I'll know if I want to swap.' Joyce was joking, but enjoyed watching Ginger roll her eyes. 'Oh, come here, give me those.' She wrestled the bundle of clothes from Ginger's arms so her friend could better manage the door. 'If that cleaner hasn't reappeared once we've had a look round, we should take some extra lotions and shower gel. They never leave enough.'

The door opened into a short corridor. As soon as they walked in, they were confronted by a portrait of Mary, giving them the once-over before they went any further. A slim woman with red-gold hair and pale skin, she was standing wearing a black dress, a hand on a wooden table and long curtains behind her. The table was a distinctly orange shade, while the curtains looked as if they should have been a kind of gold, but light bouncing off them made them also appear orange.

It was this colour that had been chosen as a key feature of the room. They stepped in and were presented with a richly decorated seating area. Fat orange velvet armchairs were set against the backdrop of William Morris-style wallpaper, which made it look fussy but welcoming. A stone bust of Mary sat on the coffee table. Long orange silk curtains, reflecting the colours in the painting of Mary, framed a large window. The remaining walls were cream velveteen.

As the two women stepped further into the room, they could see how large it was. Joyce went to examine the bathroom, until her inspection was interrupted by Ginger yelping.

'Dear God!'

'What is it?' asked Joyce idly, wondering if Ginger had come face to face with a workman, or the missing cleaner had taken her by surprise. Joyce was more interested in the bathroom, which she rather liked. A roll-top bath sat in the centre of the room, the orange tiles surrounding it warming, whereas the colour in the main room was far too dark for her liking, although certainly luxurious. She had a look at the toiletries: a very nice, and expensive, locally produced brand. She was definitely going to be raiding the housekeeper's trolley and more than once.

'JOYCE! Where the hell are you?'

'What's wrong?' Joyce made her way out of the bathroom and to the hidden half of the bedroom, which was dominated by an ornate wooden four-poster bed, patterns in the wood picked out in gold. 'Just dump your stuff and we'll go next door.'

'You don't need to worry about the cleaner catching you nicking her stuff,' Ginger declared, stepping out of the way and pointing at the bed.

'Why? Oh…' Following the direction of Ginger's finger, Joyce saw a woman dressed in black lying on the sheets. She strode towards the prone figure. 'Sleeping on the job? There'll be no tip for her.'

'I think she's dead, Joyce. In fact, I'm sure she is.'

Joyce stopped suddenly, not keen to get too close to a corpse, but still she leaned over, seeing red marks lining the woman's neck.

'I'll call reception.' She picked up the phone by the bed and dialled 0.

'Hang on one minute.' Ginger sounded curious. 'That's not a cleaner's uniform. That's Mary, Queen of Scots. Oh my goodness, I made her dress. I know her.'

Get your copy of *Murder En Suite* to join Joyce and Ginger for a luxurious break, with laughs aplenty and mysteries to solve everywhere you turn.

READ A FREE CHARLETON HOUSE MYSTERY

Building a relationship with my readers is one of the best things about writing. I occasionally send newsletters with details on new releases, special offers, interviews and articles relating to The Charleton House Mysteries.

Sign up to my mailing list and you'll also receive the very first Charleton House Mystery, *A Stately Murder*.

Head to my website for your free copy and find out what happens when Sophie stumbles across the victim of the first murder Charleton House has ever known.

www.katepadams.com

ABOUT THE AUTHOR

After 25 years working in some of England's finest buildings, Kate P. Adams has turned to murder.

Kate grew up in Derbyshire, the setting for many of her books, and went on to work in theatres around the country, the Natural History Museum - London, the University of Oxford and Hampton Court Palace. Every day she explored darkened corridors and rooms full of history behind doors the public never get to enter. Kate spent years in these beautiful buildings listening to fantastic tales, wondering where the bodies were hidden, and hoping that she'd run into a ghost or two.

Kate has an unhealthy obsession with finding the perfect cup of coffee, enjoys a gin and tonic, and is managed by Pumpkin, a domineering tabby cat who is a little on the large side. Now that she lives in the USA, writing The Charleton House Mysteries allows Kate to go home to her beloved Derbyshire everyday, in her head at least.

ACKNOWLEDGEMENTS

My talented editor Alison Jack, and Julia Gibbs, my eagle-eyed proofreader. It is always a pleasure to work with them.

I'm extremely grateful to Richard Mason, my police advisor who guides me on procedure and makes sure I am, largely, within the law. When I break the rules, that's all me!

Julie Chapman of Charlie Foxtrot Typewriters, for helping me with the finer details of the Imperial No. 1 typewriter.

Jo Orme, who made sure I had enough coffee to get to the end of this project.

Laura Weatherly for being #teamkate

Thank you to my readers for your patience.

Printed in Great Britain
by Amazon